# Blitz

# Blitz

By

**Sue Perkins**

**Desert Breeze Publishing, Inc.**
27305 W. Live Oak Rd #424
Castaic, CA 91384

http://www.DesertBreezePublishing.com

Copyright © 2011 by Sue Perkins
ISBN 10: 1-61252-895-3
ISBN 13: 978-1-61252-895-3

Published in the United States of America
Electronic Publish Date: May 2011
Print Publish Date: June 2013

Editor-In-Chief: Gail R. Delaney
Content Editor: Sandra Sookoo
Marketing Director: Jenifer Ranieri
Cover Artist: Jenifer Ranieri

Cover Art Copyright by Desert Breeze Publishing, Inc © 2011

## Other Books by Sue Perkins

*Three Hearts*
*Recipe for Romance*
*The Sixth Key*

*Dragon Flame*
*Dragon Clans*
*Dragon Fire*

# Dedication

Blitz is dedicated to the memory of my parents Vera and Geoffrey.
Their love story provided the inspiration for this book.

# Chapter One

*May 1938*

"Florence, are you there?" Velma knocked on the door. No answer. She pushed it open and called again. "It's only me."

She heard a muffled noise in the kitchen at the back of the house and grinned. Her sister must be busy with little Sam. Florence's life centered on the four-year-old. Everything faded into the background when she and Sam were alone. Velma moved down the hallway and pushed open the door at the end.

Sunshine filled the kitchen and blinded her for a moment. She stretched her arms out wide to welcome the warmth and twirled round and round, the skirt of her cotton print frock flaring as she spun. Velma stopped abruptly. The other person in the room definitely wasn't her sister. Dark eyes watched her. Male eyes full of amusement had followed her carefree dance.

"Who are you?" Her voice sounded breathless. She stopped, facing him.

"I might ask you the same question."

Velma tilted her head to one side as she considered the man in front of her. He'd made himself at home. The warmth of the kitchen had encouraged him to take off his khaki jacket and drape it over the back of a chair. He wore no shirt. The startling white of his vest stood out against his sunburned arms. Black braces attached to the waistband of his trousers had been released from his shoulders and looped down to accentuate the slim hips. Tendrils of hair on his chest escaped the top of the vest and Velma shivered as a tingle crept through her body.

She had to raise her head to see his face as he stood several inches taller than her. His dark hair had been combed to one side with a precise straight parting, and his face showed a deeper tan than his arms. Her gaze shifted to his twinkling dark brown eyes.

"Like what you see?"

"I'd like it better if I had a name to put to the face. Who are you?"

"Ladies first." His infectious grin made Velma respond with a smile of her own.

"I'm Velma, Florence's sister, and you are..."

"Jack. George's brother."

One of Florence's brothers-in-law. Now she knew his identity she could see the resemblance to George. Several of the Stanley brothers had attended Florence's wedding some years ago. She couldn't remember Jack. Both bride and groom came from large families so the church and reception had been pretty crowded.

"Where's Florence?"

"She took little Sam to meet his daddy off the bus." Jack picked up the kettle and filled it from the tap over the sink. "Can I make you a cup of tea?"

"That would be nice."

Velma watched him through lowered lashes as he turned the gas on and struck a match to light the hob. He placed the large kettle over the flames.

"Tell me about yourself."

He emptied the dregs from the teapot. "Not much to tell. I'm younger than George. Joined the RASC a few years ago."

"RASC? Sorry, I don't know what that is."

"Royal Army Service Corps. I'm a driver and mechanic. There's not much work on Hayling Island. I've always been interested in engines and motor vehicles, so I headed straight for the transport section when I joined."

"Aren't you worried about being in the armed services? My brother says there's a war brewing. Germany is trying to grab more than its fair share of land."

"Worried? I'm not sure what you mean. Do you think I'm afraid to fight for my king and country?" He frowned at her, annoyance flashed in his eyes.

*Oh heavens, he thinks I'm questioning his bravery!*

"Of course that's not what I think," she hastened to explain. "But don't you get a bit frightened you might have to fight. Kill or be killed? I know it would scare me to death."

"There wouldn't be a problem then would there?"

Velma relaxed as Jack grinned and his anger evaporated. He poured hot water into the teapot, swirled it round and emptied it into the sink. Returning the pot to the draining board, he put in three spoonfuls of tea and poured on hot water.

"We'll leave it to draw for a few moments." He placed the teapot on the table, followed by cups, saucers, tea strainer and milk jug. "Do you take sugar?"

"No thanks."

Velma ducked her head to hide her flush of embarrassment. Letting him make her a cup of tea indicated a closeness to each other. She considered Florence's house a second home. She should have been the one to make the pot of tea. To relieve the tension building up inside her she searched for something to say.

"Tell me about Hayling Island. George's spoken of it often. I've never been there."

"Not much to tell really." He poured tea into the cups. "It's a small island just off the coast near Portsmouth. George and I grew up there, along with the rest of our brothers and our sister. My brother Will and I are the same age. He's a postman on the island."

"I know who you are," Velma exclaimed. "You're one of the twins, the youngest one."

"People always call me the youngest." Jack laughed. "Will's only twenty minutes older than me."

"What's it like having someone who's identical to you?"

"It's nice when you're growing up. We always had someone our own age to play with. We looked alike so we played lots of tricks on people. Coming from such a big family having a playmate made all the difference, especially as our sister is the youngest. She got spoiled by everyone. Will and I are nearly thirty now and we've got different ideas on what we want to do, but we're still close."

"I know what you mean about big families," Velma sighed. "We've got the same amount as you. Ours is the other way round. Eight girls and one boy. I'm the baby of the family and at times it's not nice."

"Don't you get spoiled?"

Jack blew on his tea before taking a sip and the same warm shiver rushed through Velma's body. She liked this man a lot, he made her feel relaxed. The comfort made more acute by the thrill of excitement at being so near to him.

"Yes, I've been spoiled," she admitted. "But I also get overprotected. My sisters and their husbands think it's their duty to take care of me. They forget I'm nearly twenty-five and quite capable of taking care of myself. My older sisters have been watching over me for so long I guess it's difficult for them to remember I'm all grown up."

"You look like a full grown woman to me."

Jack's reached out and touched her hand. Warmth passed between them; warmth that promised a wealth of feelings for the future.

"We're ba-ack."

Velma snatched her hand away at Florence's call. Little Sam came running down the hallway, followed by his parents.

"Aunty Vee. Aunty Vee." The boy threw himself into her arms and Velma smiled. He never could say her name properly. She quite liked his version.

"Hello, Velma." Florence gave her a hug. "When did you get here? Has Jack been taking care of you?"

"Yes, he has." Velma indicated the empty cups on the table. "You didn't tell me George's brother had come to visit."

"My fault," Jack interrupted. "I had some leave owing and decided to come and see my brother and his family. I arrived unannounced on their doorstep last night."

"We're glad you did," Florence removed her hat from her shining auburn hair. "It's lovely to see you. George doesn't get to see his own family very often. Are you staying for tea, Velma? It's only salad and cold meats."

"I'll stay if it's all right with you?"

"Of course it is. You can help me get everything ready. George will you keep an eye on Sam for me?"

George lifted Sam onto his lap where the boy cuddled into his father's chest. The sisters smiled.

"He's so good with him," Florence told Velma as they washed the salad ingredients and placed them in the bowl. "And Sam adores him."

"His brother's quite nice." Velma covertly glanced at Jack.

"You sound interested." Florence smiled at her younger sister. "Wouldn't that be nice two brothers with two sisters?"

"Hey, you're jumping the gun. We've only just met."

"Don't worry, I'm teasing." Florence picked up the plate of buttered bread, each slice neatly cut into halves. "Bring the cold meat would you."

"This looks nice, dear," George commented as Florence placed some salad and meat on her son's plate.

"Thank you."

Velma watched Florence smile at her husband. *That's the sort of marriage I want. A husband who appreciates what I do and who doesn't think it's wrong to thank me out loud.*

"Could you pass the bread and butter please?"

Jack's request broke into her reverie. Velma smiled as she held the plate for him while he took three pieces.

"What do you think about the chances of there being a war?" George asked and Velma held her breath as she waited for Jack's answer. War. The last thing she wanted to happen now she'd met someone she'd like to know better.

"Do you mean Hitler?" George nodded and Jack continued. "I hope not. Spain's in a mess with Franco seizing power. News from Russia is a bit of a worry. Stalin seems to be house cleaning his top brass in the Russian Army."

"How will that affect us?" Velma couldn't understand how upsets in these foreign countries could bring war to England.

Jack turned to smile at Velma, his teeth brilliant white against his suntanned face. "We've got agreements with a lot of the little countries around Russia and Germany. If they're attacked we'll go to their aid."

Velma shivered. She didn't want to hear about war. If she tried to change the subject would Jack think her shallow?

"Do you think war is definitely coming? When do you think it will happen?"

"Don't worry, Velma," Jack smiled again. "I doubt if it will happen this year, or even next. The powers-that-be may come to their senses and do something to stop Hitler's agenda."

Velma wished they would stop talking about war. She didn't want to think of the men in her family going off to fight. Why couldn't everything stay the same?

Little Sam upset his glass of water and his mother hastened to clean up the mess. In the confusion she saw Jack glance at her. He abruptly changed the subject to the unusually warm weather.

Twenty minutes later Sam went off to bed. For the next few hours the adults sat outside discussing family news and enjoying several pots of tea.

"It's getting late." Velma hid a yawn behind her hand. "I should be heading home."

"It's dark now, Velma; you shouldn't go on your own. Jack will walk with you." Florence frowned. "Don't dawdle on the way or Josie will worry about you."

Velma opened her mouth to say she could see herself home perfectly well thank you. Luckily, she had second thoughts before she spoke. It would be so romantic to walk home under the stars with a handsome man at her side.

Jack took her arm as they walked down the street. For a while they moved in silence-but Velma knew she must eventually say something. She glanced at his face. In profile she saw his rounded chin and the five o'clock shadow on his cheeks. "So when do you have to go back to -- where is it you're stationed?"

"Aldershot," he replied. "I've got until next Wednesday. I'd like to spend some time with you. Is that all right?"

"I'd like that." She ducked her head to hide the excitement surging through her.

"Would you like to go to the pictures one night? Tomorrow perhaps?"

"That would be lovely. Saturday night there's usually a good film on. I think this week it's *Pygmalion*."

"Shall I pick you up from work tomorrow?"

"The store shuts at midday on Saturday. You can pick me up at home if you like. Come for tea." Velma fervently hoped Josie wouldn't mind her inviting a strange man to the evening meal. She would explain Jack's relationship to Florence, making him practically family.

"I've got a better idea." Jack patted the hand resting on his arm. "You go home from work and freshen up. I'll call for you then we can go for a walk in the park and have tea in a café before we go to the cinema."

For a few moments they carried on in silence. At ease with Jack, Velma could almost believe she'd known him for ever. Above them the silvery twinkle of the stars relieved the blackness of the clear sky. "I love watching the heavens." She shivered, not with the cold. Jack misunderstood and his arm moved to her shoulders, pulling her close.

"They're beautiful." Jack stared at her face and she knew he didn't mean the stars. "Almost as beautiful as you."

Velma ducked her head as warmth flooded her cheeks. The contact between them comforted and excited her. Little tingles shot up and down her body leaving a pool of excitement in her stomach. Why did this man affect her so much when she'd only known him a few short hours?

"We're here." Disappointment washed over her as they stopped outside a neat terraced house with a small garden between the house and the road. The walk from Florence's had taken a lot less time than usual.

"Is this where you live?"

"I grew up here with my sister Josie and her husband Tom. They took care of us younger children when Dad died." She opened the gate. "I expect you've heard Mum couldn't cope with so many of us on her own. I'm the only single one now. My next oldest sister got married last year."

Velma heard her voice prattling on and hoped Jack didn't think her silly. The admission of being single slipped out before she could help it. She could have kicked herself. He'd probably think her on the lookout for a husband. She'd love to go out on a date with him. It would be awful if she put him off before they'd had chance to get to know one another better.

Happiness and nervousness surged through her when Jack put his hands on her shoulders and turned her to face him. She waited breathlessly as he gazed deep into her eyes.

Slowly, he lowered his head. His lips brushed lightly against her mouth. Excitement rushed through her body from the touch of his hand stroking the back of her neck. Elation made Velma feel she floated on air. She hadn't thought he could hold her any closer. Jack tightened his arms and the kiss deepened. Lack of breath and over stimulation of her senses made her dizzy. Jack released her and Velma almost stumbled. Pulling slightly back he smiled down at her.

"I'll pick you up here tomorrow afternoon. Sleep well."

She watched him walk down the street until he turned a corner and went out of sight. Velma didn't have to glance in a mirror to know she had a soppy smile on her face. She didn't care. Jack made her feel wonderful.

Josie and Tom had already gone to bed. Velma crept quietly up the stairs, although she knew Josie would still be awake. Her older sister wouldn't settle until she knew Velma had come home.

Velma found it hard to sleep. Visions of Jack invaded her mind. Could such a handsome man really like her as much as she liked him? She went over and over the time she'd spent with him today until she could recall every single detail. She wriggled excitedly. She looked forward to tomorrow. Velma punched her pillow to settle the lumps she'd made with her tossing and turning.

*If I don't get to sleep soon I'll look like an old hag when he comes to pick me up.*

Her eyes closed at last and sleep overtook her. Dreams invaded her unconscious mind. She floated into the cinema on his arm. He waited for her to sit before he settled beside her. His arm draped across her shoulders at the start of the film. Of course he'd be too much of a gentleman to kiss her in the crowded cinema. Instead his eyes told her how much he longed to hold her in his arms again. Irritation rose in Velma's chest as the angry sound of the fire alarm interrupted the film.

Velma struggled awake. She lay in her bed and instead of a fire alarm the clanging came from her bedside clock protesting loudly. Time for her to get up. She yawned and reluctantly swung her legs off the bed.

*****

Jack walked back to George's house with his hands in his pockets. Luckily, his feet knew where he headed as he didn't pay any attention to his route. Visions of Velma filled his mind. He'd had a few girlfriends, casual and uncomplicated relationships, yet Velma affected him in a way he'd never experienced before. He couldn't get her dark wavy hair, her sparkling blue eyes or her happy smile out of his mind.

*I must have met her before. Both of us were at George and Florence's wedding.*

His forehead wrinkled as he thought about his brother's wedding day. There had been a lot of family members from both sides. The family of the groom had travelled from Hampshire whereas the bride's family all came from the Plymouth area. Consequently, more of Florence's relatives were in evidence than from George's side.

No. He couldn't recall seeing Velma then realised she would have been five years younger at that time. Florence had decided not to have bridesmaids as there were so many sisters and nieces to consider. Rather than disappoint anyone she'd had her only brother lead her down the aisle with no other attendants.

He reached out to open George's front door and smiled. He might not have remembered her from their previous meeting but he certainly wouldn't forget Velma Field now. If he had his way the beautiful woman he'd met tonight would be Mrs. Jack Stanley in the not too distant future.

*****

"You seem happy." Gladdie looked at her suspiciously.

"I am, Gladdie, I'm very happy. I've met someone." Velma gave a little skip of joy and then apologised as she tripped over her friend's feet.

"He must be something special if he makes you act like this." Gladdie laughed setting her dark curls bobbing. Velma could tell by the eager expression on her friend's face that she wanted to know more. "Who is he?"

"You know Florence's husband, George?"

"Yes. What's he got to do with you meeting someone?"

"It's his younger brother, Jack."

"Jack. Which one is he?" Gladdie held the store's rear door open and the two of them passed through. They continued talking as they climbed the stairs to the staff changing room.

"One of the twins; the youngest brother. The only one younger than him in his family is his sister, Grace."

"Does that mean there's another one just like him out there for me?"

Gladdie's green eyes sparkled.

"His twin Will? Yes, they're identical. I think he's already taken."

"Shame. So tell me, what does this handsome hunk do?"

"He's in the Royal Army Service Corps. He's a driver in the transport division. He's so handsome in his uniform." Velma smiled as a vision of Jack's face floated across her mind.

"Talking of uniforms, we'd better hurry and put ours on or we'll be late on the sales floor."

Velma grabbed her dress by the hem, pulled it over her head and dropped it on the seat. She slipped her arms through the sleeves of her store overall and buttoned it over her slip, then hung her dress on the hanger. Arm in arm the two friends raced down the stairs to the sales floor of the large store and hurried to their counters. Mrs Harris, the supervisor, stood next to the hardware counter, her eyes flicking from the clock hanging from the high ceiling to the young women hurrying to their stations. Velma slipped in behind the counter as the opening bell rang.

At morning break the two women grabbed their cups of tea and hurried onto the flat roof area to sit under the clear blue sky. They only had a fifteen minute break and intended to make the most of the sunshine.

"So tell me more about this Jack of yours." Gladdie took a sip of her tea.

"He's got dark hair, dark eyes, a gorgeous tan and he's really nice." Velma stared dreamily, her eyes seeing Jack instead of the area around her.

"So are you going to go out with him?"

"He walked me home from Florence's last night, and he's asked me to the cinema tonight. We're going out for tea first."

Jack's goodnight kiss floated to the surface of her mind. Should she tell Gladdie? No. She wanted to keep the wonderful memory to herself for now.

"What picture are you going to see?"

"*Pygmalion*. Leslie Howard's in it and he's gorgeous."

"Like Jack?" Gladdie grinned and Velma punched her lightly in the arm.

"No silly. Jack's real. Leslie Howard is a film star who wouldn't even notice the likes of me."

"So is this Jack picking you up from work?"

"I'm going home to change first, then Jack said he'd call for me. We're going for a walk then we'll have tea in a café before going to the cinema."

"Oh, very posh. Are you sure his twin's taken?"

Before Velma could answer, the warning bell rang loudly to tell the staff the time had come to return to work.

At midday Velma rushed through her cashing up and ran up the stairs to get changed. She almost knocked Gladdie over in her haste to leave the cloakroom and return home.

"Calm down, Velma. If you carry on at this rate you'll be all hot and flustered by the time he picks you up."

Velma grinned, but didn't stop. She lived just outside of the main city centre and it usually took her twenty minutes to walk home. Today she ran all the way. She flung open the front door and the hall clock showed she'd left work only ten minutes before.

"Velma, slow down." Josie emerged from the kitchen wiping her hands on a towel. "Whatever's got you in such a lather?"

"Sorry. Can't stop. I'm going out for tea and then to the pictures. I'll probably be home late."

She charged up the stairs, Josie's voice floating up behind her.

"Who are you going out with? Gladdie? Velma..."

She slammed the door of her room behind her, cutting off Josie's strident queries. Her clothes quickly fell from her body until she stood naked before the mirror. Velma poured water into the china wash basin and lathered up her flannel with her best lavender soap. Feeling much fresher, she put on clean underwear then searched through her meagre wardrobe to select a dress. The sun shining through the window influenced her choice and she picked a floral print sundress. She brushed her hair, powdered her face and carefully put on bright red lipstick. Standing back she blotted her lips and smiled at herself in the mirror to make sure no lipstick smudges stained her teeth.

Excitement made her unsure if she'd made the right decision regarding her dress.

*Gracious, if I carry on like this I won't be ready when Jack comes.*

Velma couldn't help it. She did a little dance then took a moment to scrutinise her reflection. Her dark hair shone with the intensive brushing she had given it, and her blue eyes glowed with happiness. She'd got the right amount of powder on her face and for once the lipstick had gone where it should go, instead of outside the line of her lips. The dress had been the right choice. It showed off her figure to perfection.

A knock on the front door announced the arrival of Jack. Heart pounding and with stomach churning Velma gave a final pat to her hair. She grabbed her clutch bag and hurried down the stairs.

# Chapter Two

"Velma's expecting me." Jack smiled at the woman who had opened the door. He assumed this to be the sister, Josie.

"Come in. Come in." Josie moved back to let him enter.

Jack stepped over the threshold and Velma's sister smiled at him. He heard a noise above and glanced up. Velma stood at the bend of the stairs smiling tremulously at him and Jack returned the grin.

*She's so beautiful.* His heart filled with pride such a wonderful woman had agreed to go out with him.

"I'll put the kettle on." Josie turned towards the kitchen. "You've time for a cup of tea before you go, haven't you?"

Jack raised an eyebrow in Velma's direction. Did she want this? He didn't want to appear rude and breathed a silent sigh of relief when Velma took matters into her own hands.

"Sorry Josie, we don't have time. Oh, do you two know one another? Josie this is George's brother Jack. Jack this is my sister Josie."

"I think we met at George's wedding. It's nice to see you again, Josie. Perhaps we could have the tea some other time."

"Of course." Josie responded to his apology with a nod of her head. "Have a good time you two."

Moments later the front door shut behind them. As they walked down the street Jack took Velma's hand and his finger brushed across her palm. She blushed but didn't attempt to pull away.

"Do you want to go anywhere in particular?"

"We could go for a walk on the Hoe."

"Sounds good to me. Why don't you lead the way?"

*****

Velma liked the way he tucked her arm through his, it sent a warm glow through her and made her feel cherished and respected at the same time. They walked through the streets leading up to Plymouth Hoe. The huge gates opened onto the brow of the land and she turned to face Jack as he whistled in surprise.

"Wow, this is great!" He glanced around with an amazed expression on his face. "So much space."

A long tarmac promenade stretched before them with wide expanses of grass on either side.

"This isn't all there is. There's a new lido on the sea front." Velma said.

"What's that over there?" Jack pointed to a column supported by four corner buttresses.

"It's the War Memorial." She led the way towards the monument. "They built it to commemorate the naval dead of the Great War. See the four ship prows branching out of the top. They're supposed to represent the four winds."

"The four winds?"

Jack smiled and for a moment irritation rose up inside of Velma. Did he think she had no true idea of the purpose of the monument? This particular edifice had special meaning for her family.

"I would have thought growing up on an island you would know about the winds. There's the angry north wind, the fair south, the cruel east and the kindly west. The copper ball on top represents the globe." She counted to ten to calm herself. Jack would have no idea of the significance of the memorial. His smile had been for her, not what she'd said.

"Do all the naval dead have their names on there?" His voice had softened and he smiled gently at her.

Velma knew Jack had seen her annoyance and he now tried to make amends.

"There are about seven thousand names on there, and the names of the battles they were killed in. See the inscription."

She had read it so many times before she knew the words by heart, and she spoke them in her mind as Jack read them,

"In honour of the Navy and to the abiding memory of those ranks and ratings of this Port who laid down their lives in the defence of the Empire and have no other grave than the sea."

Velma wandered over and let her fingers trace one of the names on the bronze plaques.

"Someone you know?" Jack asked.

"My father, Philip Samuel Field," she read the inscription. "He died on the *HMS Indefatigable*. His ship sank in the Battle of Jutland."

Tears pricked her eyes, but she took a deep breath to compose herself.

"I'm sorry. I knew he'd died. No one told me the details." Jack's voice had softened.

"I'd just had my second birthday when his ship went down. My mother didn't take it too well. Josie thinks she found it more difficult without a body to bury. Mum needed continuous medical treatment afterwards so I really lost both my parents at the same time." A shiver passed through Velma's body. She turned to Jack, gripping his arm hard. "You don't really think there will be another war do you?"

"I'd like to say no, but it wouldn't be the truth." Jack looked deep into her eyes. "For some reason the world goes mad every now and then. The result is war. All the signs point to there being some sort of conflict in the next few years."

"And you'll go and fight, won't you?" The tears pricked her eyes.

"It's my duty, Velma," Jack said quietly. "If war starts, I'll be proud to go and do my bit."

She took one last look at her father's name before turning her back on the memorial. No matter how many times she visited this place, it still made her feel sad. She wondered how different her life would have been if her father had survived the Great War.

"Let me show you the rest of the Hoe."

Arm in arm they walked along the promenade and Velma pointed out the various sights.

"There's the bandstand and--"

"Is that a lighthouse?" Jack's eyes opened wide. "What's a lighthouse doing up here? Shouldn't it be out at sea?"

"It used to be. They brought Smeaton's Tower in from the Eddystone Rocks when they put a new light out there. It's quite a landmark."

Hands clasped they stood beside the tower gazing out over the turquoise sea towards the breakwater. Jack released her hand and put his arm around her shoulders, pulling her towards him. Warmth and comfort spread through her again, confirming her belief she and Jack were meant to be together. Velma leaned her head against his chest, immediately below his shoulder.

"It's glorious here."

Through her contact with him Velma heard the rumble of his voice in his chest.

"The army and navy hold displays on the promenade sometimes. It's lovely. Most of the town turns out to enjoy the music and the marching." Velma smiled. "Last time Florence and I brought Sam to see them. He got so excited we thought he'd never go to bed that night."

They wandered along the promenade, reached the end and turned to retrace their steps. Velma wondered if Jack could read her mind. He knew her thoughts and feelings as soon as she did. He made her feel cherished. No man had ever had this effect on her before. Could it really be love?

"Did I see a café near the entrance to the Hoe? Shall we have tea there?"

"The Tea Pavilion? They only do cakes and sandwiches."

"Did you have any lunch?" Velma shook her head. "We'd better have something more substantial then."

"There'll be more choice if we go down into the town. Several cafés serve light meals." Velma heard the nervousness in her voice. She had no idea what sort of eating place Jack could afford.

"Oh, I haven't shown you the lido." Velma exclaimed as they left the Hoe through the centre gates.

"I hope we're going to have lots of outings like this. The lido will be something to see next time."

A small acorn of warmth blossomed deep inside her. She believed he shared the feelings she had for him. An intense comfort flowed through her whole body and she beamed at Jack. He'd stopped to take in the view of the buildings below.

"This is wonderful. You can see the whole of the city from here."

"You could if the rooftops didn't block the view," Velma commented. "But you're right, it is spectacular."

When they arrived in the centre of the city Velma led the way down the main street past several cafés.

"How about this one?" Jack indicated a small restaurant with a bow fronted window. Wooden frames divided the window into squares; some of them were bottle glass.

"It's nice." Velma almost sighed with relief. She'd been afraid he might take her to some place where her summer frock would be totally out of place.

Jack held the door open for her and she hid her surprise. None of the young men she knew did this for anyone except for the older women in their families. Her sisters' husbands and her brother did it automatically for the women in their lives. She'd thought it a thing specific to her family.

They settled in a table by the window and Velma took an interest in her surroundings. She'd never been in this particular eatery before. The inside of the café at first appeared dark. Her eyes soon got used to the dim light. The difference lay between the strong sunshine outside and the twilight-style interior. Neat round tables covered with checked cloths dotted the room with wooden chairs tucked under each table.

The waitress approached, order book and pen in her hand as she waited for them to decide.

"Would you like egg and chips?" Jack asked. "That should keep us going until we go to the cinema."

"Sounds lovely." Velma made a mental note to eat slowly and make sure the egg yolk didn't drip down her chin.

The service proved quick and efficient, within five minutes two plates piled high with chips and two eggs apiece were placed in front of them. Velma's eyes widened in horror. She'd been brought up to 'waste not, want not'. She'd never be able to get through all this. Valiantly, she picked up her knife and fork and prepared to attack the food.

"You can leave whatever you don't have room for."

Velma glanced at Jack. He smiled. He must have been watching the emotions flit across her face. He'd guessed the thoughts passing through her mind.

"It's just so -- so much." Velma smiled at him. "Do you want any of these chips?"

"I don't think so," he replied. "I've got my own pile to deal with."

Silence reigned for several minutes while they ate their meal. Jack had also ordered a pot of tea and this arrived as they decided they were full. Velma had eaten both eggs and about half the chips. Jack had managed two thirds of his plateful. The waitress shook her head as she removed their plates. As the woman walked away Velma saw Jack grinning from ear to ear. She put her hand over her mouth to smother a laugh.

"I think we're in disgrace but you have to admit we did our best."

"Shall I pour?" Velma didn't wait for a reply.

She picked up the milk and poured it into their cups then checked the tea had drawn properly. As she sipped her eyes watched Jack over the rim of her cup. At first his eyes were full of amusement then slowly they became sombre. He placed his cup on the saucer and she did the same. His hand reached across and enfolded hers, large fingers folding over her knuckles. She'd always had small hands. The pure white against his tanned skin made them look even tinier and more delicate.

"You do know how I feel about you don't you, Velma?"

"I -- I'm not sure. I hope you feel the same way as I feel about you." She managed to say.

"I think I've fallen in love with you. No darn it, I know I've fallen in love with you. Please don't be frightened," he quickly added as she tried to withdraw her hand. "I'm not going to rush you, Velma. We'll take it at your pace. I want to see you as much as possible before I have to go back to Aldershot."

A tremor of fright rocketed through at his words. Too much, too soon. They'd only met properly yesterday. The words imprinted on her mind and she wondered what frightened her. If she looked deep inside herself she had the same spark of love for him.

"I'm just a bit scared we might be going too fast, Jack. I think I've fallen in love with you too. How do I know it's the real thing? I've got nothing to compare it to. I've never been in love before."

"Good." He smiled at her shocked expression. "That means your feelings for me are one of a kind. I hate to think you've had these feelings for any other man."

"Have you ever -- I mean..."

"Loved another woman? No, I haven't. I knew as soon as I met you yesterday you were the woman I wanted to spend the rest of my life with. I think it's called love at first sight. I've never believed in it before. I do now." Jack's thumb caressed the palm of her hand and a shiver of excitement rippled out from his touch.

"Maybe we should leave it at that. It's time we were going. The film starts soon."

Jack paid the bill and held the door open for her as they left. Arms linked they walked slowly down the road to the cinema.

*He's not only really handsome, he's also a perfect gentleman.* Velma grinned as Jack paid for their tickets then led her over to the confectionery counter. For a moment her disappointment rose when Jack didn't head for the back row of the cinema. She'd assumed they would miss most of the film as they kissed and cuddled in the darkness. This had happened on previous visits

14

with the youths she'd known since childhood. Instead, Jack led the way half-way down the aisle where he stood to one side to let her enter the row before him. Once they were seated he handed her the bag of chocolates he'd purchased in the foyer and she smiled her thanks.

*****

The lights dimmed and Jack reached over to capture Velma's hand. He wondered if she'd been disappointed they weren't sitting in the back row, the obvious spot for young lovers. He had considered it, but decided he couldn't take the risk. He wanted this woman for his wife. You didn't kiss and cuddle in a public place with such an important person. She deserved much more respect than a quick fumble in the dark.

The screen flickered for the start of film. He expected to be bored by what he considered to be a woman's film. To his surprise he caught himself enjoying it, even laughing when the young Eliza Doolittle got everything so spectacularly wrong.

"Would you like an ice cream?" He turned to Velma when the lights came up at intermission.

"Thank you, no. I'm still full from the enormous tea we had. I haven't eaten any of the chocolates yet. You have one if you want."

"I'm not hungry either, but I wondered if you were."

They smiled at each other and he could imagine the voice of his friend Pete telling him he looked really daft. He didn't care. Velma made him feel the happiest he'd been in a long time.

*****

Velma sighed as the final credits crawled up the screen. The lights came up and people stood to leave the cinema.

"Did you enjoy the film?"

"Mmm, wonderful." She still dwelt in the world of *Pygmalion* and her words were dreamy. Jack touched her elbow and she turned to smile at him. "Thank you. I don't think I've ever enjoyed an evening so much."

A light rain fell as they left the cinema. Jack put his arm round her shoulders.

"Do you want to take shelter somewhere, or shall we try and dodge the raindrops?"

"I think the pubs are the only places open at this time."

Velma wrinkled her nose in distaste. Decent women didn't go into drinking places except for a lemonade in the garden on a sunny afternoon. To her relief Jack understood her reluctance and turned them in the direction of home.

The rain had been affected by tiredness, too. By the time they reached the bottom of the main street the light shower had stopped and the stars broke through the cloudy sky. Jack slid his arm from her shoulders and took her hand instead.

"Velma, would you come for a ride with me tomorrow? Florence says you can hire bikes from the shop near your house. I'd really like for us to go bike riding and perhaps stop somewhere for high tea."

The Field family weren't very religious. They tried to keep Sunday as a family day. She didn't know how her sisters would react if she announced she would be going out on a Sunday afternoon. A solution occurred to her but she didn't know how Jack would take it.

"My sisters and their families call in on a Sunday afternoon. I don't think they'd say anything if I went for a bike ride. Would you mind if we went back to my house for tea?" She waited breathlessly for his reply.

"Of course we can eat with your family." They passed a street lamp and he smiled down at her. "I know what it's like to come from a big family. They expect you to be there for family gatherings."

They walked in comfortable silence until they stood outside Velma's front door. Jack's finger lifted her chin until she looked into his face. She could hardly breathe. Would he kiss her? Would he try to go further than a kiss, and if he did -- would she let him?

# Chapter Three

Velma slept late on Sunday morning. When she woke up she lay in her bed reliving the previous evening, enjoying every second once again. The film had been wonderful and seeing it with Jack made it extra special. Then the walk home under the stars had been so romantic.

She touched her lips. She could still feel Jack's tender kiss as he bade her goodnight. It had been quite chaste. At the same time she found it intensely emotional. Velma wanted to throw her arms around his neck, and declare her undying love for him, offering her body for his every whim. Of course she'd done none of those things. Josie would have a fit if she thought Velma had even thought of behaving in such a demeaning way.

Velma glanced at the alarm clock. She threw back the covers and jumped out of bed. The rug took the chill off the floor but as soon as she moved to the wash basin the cold linoleum attacked her toes. Her morning wash took no time at all and she'd soon dressed in slacks and light jumper, all ready to face the day.

"Morning, Josie." She placed two pieces of bread under the grill to brown.

"Good morning, Velma," her sister replied. "Did you have a nice time last night?"

"Yes, thanks. *Pygmalion* is a lovely film. You should get Tom to take you. I think you'd both enjoy it."

Velma poured herself a cup of tea and retrieved the toast. Spreading it with a scraping of butter she sat at the kitchen table to have her breakfast. She still had the previous evening on her mind and at first she didn't hear Josie speak to her.

"Velma, are you listening to me?"

"Sorry. Did you say something?"

Josie sighed and shook her head. "Honestly Velma, sometimes I think you live in a world of your own and the rest of us are just crowding round the outside. I said that Enid, Florence, Jean and their families will be here this afternoon. Do you think Jack would like to come? John said their lot might come, too."

"I've already invited Jack for tea," A flutter of excitement crossed her stomach as Velma thought of Jack. "But we're going to hire some bikes and go for a ride first."

"As long as you're back by four o'clock."

"I think I'll pop down and make sure old Mr. James keeps a couple of bikes for us. You know how popular Sunday is."

Velma made a hasty retreat to the bike shop. Mr James, an old sweetie who had a soft spot for her, promised to keep two of his best machines for Velma and her young man. She walked out of the shop and decided not to return home. Josie had a way of wheedling information out of her. She knew her sisters would dissect everything about Jack while they were out. Velma didn't want to give them further ammunition for gossip.

She smiled. They wouldn't be able to go over all Jack's good and bad points -- not that there were any bad points. George would be there and it wouldn't be polite to run his brother down. Of course this wouldn't stop them questioning George for all the details concerning the young man who took out their baby sister.

Velma's home lay quite near the Cathedral in Wyndham Square. She and her next eldest sister Fay had used the square as their playground when they were younger. Now, she walked round the area, the image of a well brought up young woman.

*Good job nobody can see inside my mind.* Velma smiled causing a passing young man to turn and stare. *All I can think of is Jack. He's so handsome and loving and caring. How could I have missed him all those years ago?*

She knew the answer without having to think about it. Five years ago she'd been a lot younger and had considered the opposite sex to be more of a nuisance than a romantic interest. Young men such as Jack wouldn't have crossed the horizon of her mind.

Down in the city one of the clock towers rang out midday. Velma turned and hurried home. She'd have to eat Sunday dinner with Josie and Tom or they'd think something had happened and wouldn't let her go with Jack. Velma shook her head. It didn't matter how old she grew, Josie still treated her like a child and she knew this wouldn't stop until she married and left home.

No conversation interrupted the meal. Velma knew from other times, Josie would be worrying about the sister's coming and Tom would be thinking of his garden. As soon as the plates were empty, Velma and Josie cleared the table. They were doing the dishes when Jack arrived. Tom sat in the yard outside the kitchen door, enjoying the afternoon sunshine.

"You go and chat to my husband while we finish up here." Josie shooed their visitor outside.

Josie turned back to the sink and Jack grinned ruefully at Velma. She could see he knew this had been planned. Tom had been delegated to question the young man to make sure they considered him a suitable escort for Velma.

*It's all rather silly really. We've only been out on one date, well two if you count the afternoon and evening separately. I do wish my family weren't so protective.*

The dishes were soon finished and Velma and Jack escaped to the bike shop. Jack had borrowed George's cycle clips and she held his machine while he clipped them round the bottom of his trousers. This done, they mounted and rode off through Wyndham Square.

"Is there anywhere in particular you'd like to go?" Velma asked.

"We could ride along the front of the Hoe and down into the Barbican. George tells me it's quite a pleasant trip and we'd have a view of the sea most of the way."

They rode side by side as they wound through the light traffic of a Sunday afternoon. Even this petered out as they reached the road running beside the wall above the sea. Many cyclists rode along enjoying a Sunday outing. Families with young children walked past on the footpath enjoying the sea air and sunshine. Velma and Jack had to concentrate as they made their way through the other cycling enthusiasts and didn't have the chance to talk. Jack eventually indicated he wanted to pull into the side.

"Isn't this a wonderful view?" He waved his hand at the sparkling sea with the breakwater on the horizon and Drakes Island closer in.

"But you must be used to seeing the sea. You live on an island."

"I can tell you've never been to Hayling Island. It's reasonably flat so you don't have the chance to climb up and look down on things. This is absolutely beautiful."

They enjoyed the view for a few more moments then continued peddling towards the Barbican. This time the way led downhill so they soon arrived at their destination. The smell from the fishing boats assailed Velma's nostrils, but she didn't mind. Another smell to cherish and remind her of her afternoon with Jack.

"Would you like an ice cream? To make up for the one we didn't have room for last night?"

"Yes, please."

Velma held the bikes while Jack purchased two cones from the ice cream stall next to one of the cafés. When he returned they wheeled their machines across the cobbles and stopped by the Mayflower Steps. They watched the comings and goings of the fishermen as they prepared their boats for their next trip out to sea.

"You do realise the family is probably tearing your reputation to pieces while we're out, don't you?" Velma had been tempted to bring up the subject all afternoon. The opportunity hadn't arisen. Now she just had to make him aware of what her sisters were doing back at the house. She couldn't let him walk into a room full of possibly hostile people.

*****

Jack smiled at the nervous woman in front of him. He longed to put his arms around her, kiss those perfect lips and run his fingers through her dark hair. Instead he licked his ice cream before he answered.

"It's all right, Velma. George warned me what would happen. He and Florence promised to stand up for me."

"Well, that's a relief. My sisters can get quite intense about me when they think I need protecting."

"And do you -- need protecting I mean?"

Velma ducked her head and he knew she'd been overcome by shyness.

"Not from you."

He had to strain to hear her low voice. His stomach churned with nerves as he prepared himself to talk to her about their future. He'd been awake half the night trying to decide if he should speak. It might be too soon. The war would definitely come in the next year or two. He wanted to be sure she understood his feelings for her before he returned to Aldershot.

"Velma, I have something to ask you. Come over here and sit down."

He led the way to a seat beside the harbour wall and leaned his bike against the rough stones, then placed hers beside it. Gently, he pulled her to sit beside him on the seat.

"Even though we've only known each other properly for two days, I meant it when I said I loved you. You've done me the honour of saying you feel the same way. I have no intention of rushing you, but I need to know if you want us to make a future together. Not immediately, sometime in the next year or so. I'd like to write to you while I'm away, and if you could write back it would be wonderful."

"Jack I--"

"Wait. I need to say something else. Velma, there's going to be a war. Not soon, but next year or maybe in two years. I want you to be my wife by the time war is declared. There won't be any question of starting a family right away. I couldn't bear it if I thought you might be left to bring up a child of ours alone. I want you to think about all of this and let me know your answer in a few weeks, or months if you need that amount of time. Will you write to me?" He watched carefully to see her reaction to his words. To his relief she smiled at him.

"Of course I will. Jack, I don't really need time to think."

"But I want you to take time." He knew she must consider everything he'd said. She had to be absolutely sure she knew what she marrying him meant. "Speak to your sisters, Florence in particular. Ask George anything you'd like to know about me. Get to know me as much as you can before you give me your answer."

*****

Velma remained silent on their ride back to Wyndham Square. Jack didn't intrude on her thoughts and she smiled gratefully at him for his understanding. They returned the bikes and walked to her home. She dreaded entering the house. The family would be there, ready and waiting to pull poor Jack to pieces. He squeezed her hand. He obviously knew what she'd been thinking. It amazed her they'd become so close in such a short time they could even sense each other's thoughts.

"Chin up," he murmured as she reached to open the door.

The nieces and nephews greeted her with delight as she and Jack entered the big front room. Her mother had kept this as the formal parlour Josie had turned it into a warm and welcoming room to accommodate most of the family when they came to visit en masse. The sisters sat round the table sipping tea and talking about their children, their homes and the local gossip. The men gathered in the kitchen discussing the more important topics of world politics and their vegetable gardens.

"Hello, everyone. This is Jack. I don't know how many of you have met him before. He's George's brother." Velma waited nervously to see how her sisters react.

All talking stopped and the women's heads turned to give Jack a detailed inspection. Velma breathed a sigh of relief as he took it all in his stride and turned on his charm.

"Good afternoon ladies. I believe I met most of you at my brother's wedding a few years ago I'm ashamed to say I can't put names to faces."

Josie hurried to make the introductions. Enid, the eldest sister, shooed Velma from the room, telling her to go and make a pot of tea.

"I'm sure the rest of us could do with a fresh cup."

Reluctantly Velma went into the kitchen and squeezed her way through the men of her family. All her sisters' husbands had accompanied them this afternoon. *I wish they'd all stop interfering. This is my life not theirs.*

She finished making the tea and took the pot back into the parlour. As she left the kitchen George winked at her, and her spirits rose. He must think Jack didn't have anything to worry about. She grinned. All the men in the kitchen had gone through the same introduction to the family when they'd begun dating their wives.

Laughter greeted her return. She wondered what they thought so funny, then she saw Jack entertaining the sisters with a story from his boyhood. Quietly she poured tea for everyone, then took her own cup and settled beside Jack. As she set her cup down he placed his hand over hers, indicating to the women the two of them were a couple.

A short while later the sisters shooed the men from the kitchen so they could begin to organise afternoon tea. Everyone had contributed food so the heavily laden table soon groaned under the weight of cold meats, salads, cakes and trifles. Velma buttered the thin slices of bread. She couldn't resist a peep into the other room. Jack sat in the thick of the talk between the men. He glanced up and looked her way with a smile. A warm glow suffused Velma and she sighed with happiness as she finished her task.

Later that evening, Velma stood outside the front door saying goodnight to Jack. They'd been for a walk in the moonlight with the full approval of the family.

"I think meeting the relatives went quite well, don't you?" Jack tucked a vagrant strand of hair behind her ear then his finger carried on to stroke her cheek.

"Well, at least you got the tick of approval." She laughed. "And you came out unscathed. I think the men were on your side. They've all been through it. I'm the youngest so you had more people interrogating you than they did."

"Goodnight my lovely Velma. I'll see you tomorrow. Shall I meet you after work?"

He didn't wait for an answer. His index finger now traced the outline of her mouth leaving a tingling sense of excitement in its wake. He bent and brushed her lips with his. Deep inside her a coiled up beast of liquid heat stirred and she shivered with anticipation. The back of his hand stroked her cheek and she leaned into his caress. Once more his lips tasted hers, delicately at first, the light touch awakening feelings totally new to her. The kisses became more intent until he put his arms around her and pulled her close to him, crushing her lips beneath his as his passion rose.

Velma melted into his embrace. Her body had a mind of its own as it responded to the tingling sensations rushing through her body. Her thoughts disappeared in a haze of emotion and she knew she wouldn't, in fact couldn't, resist no matter what he wanted to do to her. The night air cooled her cheeks and her body's excitement. She gazed up at him. She could feel her forehead crease with a frown. Why had he stopped?

"Sorry, Velma." Jack's face showed embarrassment. "I couldn't help myself. When I have you in my arms all common sense goes out the window. If I hadn't stopped then I think we would have done something we'd regret."

Velma knew he spoke the truth. She'd been in no state to take control. Thank goodness he'd been strong enough to resist the temptation they had for each other.

"So I'll wait for you tomorrow after work." He gave her forehead a chaste kiss. "See you then."

Turning abruptly, he walked off down the street. As he passed under each street lamp a halo of light surrounded his head, vanishing when he disappeared into the darkness again until he reached the next lamp. He turned and waved before he disappeared around the corner.

*****

The next day Velma hurried down the staff stairs with a smile on her lips.

"You seem happy," Gladdie commented. "Is Jack waiting for you?"

"Yes." She grinned. "We've only got a few more days so we're making the most of it."

With a final wave to her friend she burst through the door at the bottom of the stairs and out into the fresh air. Jack leaned nonchalantly against the brick wall of the building. He straightened up when Velma headed towards him.

"Ready?" He took her cardigan from her hands and placed it around her shoulders. His fingers brushed the bare skin of the top of her arms in a light caress making her shiver. She nodded and he bent and lifted a picnic basket from the ground at his feet.

"Do you realise it's our anniversary today?"

"Anniversary?" She frowned. "Anniversary of what?"

"We've been dating for three days now. I think that calls for a celebration, don't you?"

Velma's laughter rippled into the afternoon air.

"I suppose it does, but what's all this?" She flicked her hand at the basket.

"Florence says you like picnics. I thought we might go up on the Hoe and eat our food there while we watch the boats come and go."

"Why Jack, you're really quite a romantic at heart, aren't you?"

"Only when it comes to you, my love."

Jack took her hand with his free one and they strolled through the late afternoon sunshine happy to be with each other. They reached a spot near Smeaton's Tower and Jack spread a light blanket for them to sit on. She wondered how such an ordinary person as herself had been able to attract such a thoughtful, caring man.

"Only one more day, and you'll be gone, Jack." Tears sprang to her eyes and she blinked to banish them. She didn't want his memories of her to include a blotched face. "How long do you think it will be before you get leave again?"

"I'm not sure. It takes a while to get here from Aldershot so I have to make sure I have enough days off to travel this far. I've been talking to Florence and she and George want to take Sam up to see my mother on Hayling Island." He accepted a slice of cake from Velma, holding his cup ready as she poured the tea from the thermos flask. "I wondered if you'd like to go with them. I've met your family and it's only right you meet some of mine. It doesn't take long to get to there from camp. I should be able to work it so I can have a few days off and join you there. What do you think?"

Velma didn't know if she wanted to meet his mother this early in their courtship. Her spirits lifted. Florence would be with her, as well as Jack, so maybe it wouldn't be too bad. And if it meant seeing Jack again soon, she'd put up with anything.

# Chapter Four

"Can I help you?" Velma didn't glance at the customer on the other side of the counter. She concentrated on putting the last of the screws into their respective boxes.

"I hope so."

Startled by the unexpected, Velma looked up into Jack's smiling face.

"What are you doing here?" she hissed. "You'll get me into trouble."

"Sorry. I had to see you." Jack didn't seem at all sorry. How could he when he had a wide grin on his face?

"Can't it wait until lunchtime?"

The happy expression disappeared to be replaced by a worried frown. Fright rushed through Velma. What had happened to make him so unhappy?

"Can you grab a few moments? I have to speak to you."

Velma glanced around to find her supervisor. To her dismay the woman stood glaring at her from the end of the counter. The store discouraged talking to friends during working hours and Mrs. Harris followed the rules to the letter. Velma's mind desperately sought for an excuse to exchange a few words with Jack.–Nothing came immediately to mind. Jack must have seen her glance towards the supervisor. Velma watched in horror as he approached the woman. He spoke a few words to Mrs. Harris who turned to beckon to Velma.

"This young man is apparently related to your sister, Miss Field." The woman looked disbelievingly at Velma.

"Yes, Mrs. Harris. Mr. Stanley is my sister Florence's brother-in-law."

"Apparently he has an urgent message from your sister so you may take a few moments to speak to him. I shall expect you to deduct this time from your lunch hour."

"Thank you, Mrs. Harris."

Velma ducked through the counter opening and walked to the stock lift entrance where she and Jack could talk privately.

"What on earth did you say to her? There usually has to be a death in the family before she'll let any of us out from behind the counter."

"I said Florence is unwell and could you please visit her on your way home as she needs you to take care of Sam for a few hours."

"Is she really sick?" For a moment Velma forgot about Jack's sudden appearance as a flutter of anxiety surfaced regarding Florence.

"No, she's fine. She knows about this excuse so she'll play along."

"Why do you need to see me so urgently you can't wait until lunchtime?"

"I'm sorry, Velma. I received a telegram this morning. I have to report back by this evening." His hands twitched and for a moment Velma thought he would pull her to him. He didn't but his eyes showed the depth of his misery. "I'm on my way to the station now. I couldn't leave without saying goodbye."

Darkness flooded over Velma and she thought she would faint. They should have had another evening together before he had to go. Now, their last night had been snatched away from them. Desperately she tried to look and sound brave. She didn't want Jack to worry about her as he made his way back to camp.

"You will write won't you?" he pleaded. "I'll be waiting for your letters telling me all you're doing. I'm going to write to my mother to tell her all about you and we'll arrange when I can get away to coincide with your days off."

"Yes Jack, I'll write to you, but you have to promise to reply. I'm not going to send letters into a bottomless pit." She glanced over at Mrs Harris who pointed at her watch. "I have to go. Take care and have a safe journey."

It broke her heart to leave him without a kiss of farewell. She couldn't embrace him with her supervisor watching. She had to let her eyes tell him how much she loved him.

"Everything all right, Miss Field?" Mrs. Harris asked as Velma squeezed behind the counter. A glance to the lift bay told her Jack had already left.

"Yes, thank you, Mrs. Harris. Mr. Stanley wanted to make sure I visit Florence on my way home. Apparently, she's not well and needs help with my nephew."

She knew by the expression on the older woman's face Mrs. Harris had been waiting to see if her story and Jack's matched up. What little satisfaction she gained from this soon dissipated as she thought of the days ahead without Jack by her side.

*****

"What's the matter, love?"

For a moment Velma didn't speak. If she didn't talk about Jack leaving, maybe it wouldn't be true. Then the thought of the lonely months ahead overwhelmed her.

"Everything. Oh Gladdie, Jack's had to go back to camp. I don't know when I'll see him again."

"I'm so sorry, Velma." Gladdie sat beside her and put her arm around Velma's shoulders. "This doesn't mean the end of things, does it?"

"No. He's promised to write and asked me to write to him. He's going to tell his mother about me and arrange for me to visit her when Florence goes with her family. If we can work it, he'll be there at the same time. It's not far from Aldershot to Hayling Island so we'll have more time together."

"Well, that's good news isn't it? Come on Velma, chin up. Even though you've only known him a few days, Jack seems to be serious about you. How do you feel about him?"

"Oh, Gladdie. I love him. I didn't know I could possibly feel like this. Every time I see him it's like someone has let off fireworks. When he touches me my legs start to tremble and my insides feel like a volcano's erupting." Velma flushed as she confessed her feelings to her friend.

"Sounds like you've got it bad." Gladdie grinned.

"I guess so."

"Cheer up. It might not be too long before you see him again. I'd find out all you can about his mother from Florence. What she likes and dislikes, that type of thing. You need to be prepared in case she gets funny about her youngest son finding a woman to love."

Velma saw the wisdom of Gladdie's words. She should tell the truth as much as possible so she visited Florence on her way home from work.

"I hear you're not well and want help with Sam," she said with a weak grin as she walked into her sister's kitchen. "So what seems to be the problem?"

"You and Jack will get me in hot water making me part of your lies," Florence scolded. "Remind me to thank Mrs. Harris for her kindness next time I see her. Did Jack get off all right?"

"I think so." Velma ducked her head and took a deep breath. "Florence, I need your help."

"What, again? What is it now?"

"Jack says he's going to tell his mother about me and then he wants me to go with you, George and Sam next time you visit her. He's going to arrange for leave at the same time."

"That's right. He mentioned it to me. I think it's a wonderful idea. Does this mean you and I will be sisters and sister-in-laws?"

"I hope so, but it will be sometime in the future. Jack and I have to get to know one another properly first." Despite her unhappiness, a surge of excitement raced through her at the thought of spending her future with Jack.

"I don't see how you need my help with any of that. You and Jack seem to have it all worked out."

"Except I have to meet a woman I don't know, who will probably think I'm not good enough for her son. I want you to tell me all about his mother and the rest of the family."

Florence's laugh rang through the kitchen. George came through the door from the hallway and looked questioningly at his wife.

"Oh, George. Listen to this." Florence completely ignored Velma's frantic hand signals to be quiet. "Velma is worried about meeting your mother. She thinks Ma will think she's not good enough for Jack."

George grinned.

"Now, Florence, it's not nice to laugh at Velma. She probably doesn't remember my mother." He turned to face his sister-in-law. "Don't you worry about a thing Velma. Ma will love you. All she's concerned about is seeing her children lead happy lives. You could be a hunchback with a squint and it wouldn't matter. She'll be so pleased Jack's found someone to love, she'll love you for his sake."

Velma still couldn't convince herself Jack's mother would like her.

Over the next few weeks she made Florence tell her everything she could remember about the elder Mrs. Stanley. Eventually Florence called a halt to the questions.

"Enough, Velma. You're working yourself into a state about meeting Ma. She's a lovely woman. Now stop pestering me with all these questions, I'm not going to answer any more."

*****

Over the following months letters from Jack came frequently. Velma treasured each one, putting them away in a wooden jewellery box she'd received on her last birthday. She replied with equal fervour. And then the letters stopped.

At first she told herself he'd been too busy to write. Everyone talked about the European situation and no doubt the armed forces were preparing for the inevitable. Unsure of the reason for Jack's silence, Velma waited several days then wrote one more letter to him. Days passed and she still didn't hear from him.

"Velma, whatever's the matter with you?" Gladdie sounded exasperated. "You're forever snapping my head off. You're so moody nowadays."

"I am not moody," Velma stated tersely. "You're just being oversensitive."

"You're doing it now." Gladdie looked suspiciously at her. The two women were in Central Park. The ocean of green grass provided a pleasant place for a Sunday afternoon walk in the sun. They'd stopped for a rest and were sitting on a grassy mound enjoying the sunshine.

"It's Jack isn't it? What's he done -- or not done?"

Tears sprang to Velma's eyes and Gladdie put her arm around her.

"Don't cry. It can't be that bad. What's wrong?"

"He hasn't written to me for over a week now Gladdie. He's changed his mind about me, I know he has."

Now the words had been spoken at last, Velma allowed the tears to flow. Gladdie pulled her close and patted her back until the sobs subsided to hiccups.

"Silly goose." Her friend offered a clean handkerchief. "It's more likely he's busy and doesn't realise how long it is since he wrote."

Velma blew her nose and then shook her head. She leaned forward and hugged her knees.

"I knew things were too good to be true when I met him. As soon as I saw him I knew he and I were meant to be together." Velma sniffed and dabbed at her wet eyes. "When he said he wanted to marry me I couldn't believe the man I loved had the same feelings for me. He's had second thoughts now, I know it."

"Velma, do you honestly think he's the sort who would leave you hanging in the air like this? If he's changed his mind, then he'd write and tell you. Come on." Gladdie dragged Velma to her feet. "You're going home. When you get there you sit down and write to Jack and ask why he hasn't written to you."

Velma gave her friend a watery smile and arm in arm they walked towards the park entrance nearest to the route home.

*****

"Mail call."

Jack heard the announcement over the loudspeaker and eagerly lined up with the others of his troop to see if there were any letters for him. He hadn't received one from Velma for a few days and hoped there might be one from her today, or one from his mother.

"Private Jack Stanley."

He stepped forward eagerly and collected four letters. Two were in Velma's handwriting and he put these into his trouser pocket. He liked to be alone when he read her words. The others were from his mother and his brother George.

Ma first, he decided as he ripped open the envelope.

*My dear son,*

*I hope this finds you well. Thank you so much for your letter telling me of your visit to George and Florence. Your young lady sounds delightful and I look forward to seeing her when she visits with your brother's family. Hopefully you can join us at that time...*

The letter continued with news of other family members and Jack smiled as he put it in his jacket pocket. Dear old Ma. She always knew how to make her children feel special. She'd had a hard life but didn't let this get in the way of being a loving mother to her brood.

Next he opened the one sent by George and read through it quickly. His brother had never been a great letter writer and he kept his news short and to the point. George, Florence and Sam were planning to visit his mother at the end of the month. Would Jack be able to manage time off then? They hadn't seen Velma for a few days and hoped she could get the same days off. Jack shoved the letter in with his mother's and hurried over to his captain's office. Since visiting Plymouth he'd stayed in the barracks, not using any leave at all. He crossed his fingers no one else had reserved the days he wanted.

Minutes later he left the office with a broad smile on his face. The captain obviously thought of himself as cupid in disguise. He'd been only too happy to let Jack have time off to introduce his future bride to his mother.

Several hours passed until Jack could find a quiet moment to read Velma's letters. A seat beside the perimeter fence provided the privacy he needed. He opened the letter carefully, knowing the scent of lavender Velma used would exit the envelope as soon as he unstuck the flap. Jack wondered if she kept her notepad in with her soap. Whatever the reason he only had to smell lavender and Velma's face appeared in front of him.

*My darling Jack,*

*I'm so happy when I receive your letters. I miss you so much. Sometimes I feel the few days we were together were a lifetime, at other times I feel I hardly know you. One thing I do know is I can't get you out of my head – not that I want to. I'm so looking forward to seeing you again although I must confess I'm a bit nervous about meeting your mother and the rest of your family. I know now how you must have felt with my sisters watching your every move.*

*George and Florence say I'm being silly, your mother is a lovely woman and she'll make me very welcome. What if she doesn't like me?*

*I think George is intending to visit Hayling Island at the end of the month. Please, please make your captain give you the time off. I don't want to meet your family without you by my side. I can't wait to see you again...*

The letter continued with news of what Velma had been doing in the few days before she wrote and Jack smiled. He'd tell her his mother had written to say how pleased she'd be to meet her. No doubt Velma would think Ma may have said this but in reality reserved her judgement until she met Velma. Jack shook his head. If Velma wouldn't believe George and Florence, he didn't think anything he said would reassure her. He reached into his pocket for Velma's second letter. As he read the contents his happiness dissipated, leaving him with a hollow feeling inside.

*Dear Jack,*

*I haven't heard from you for over a week and I'm wondering if something is wrong. If you've had second thoughts I would rather know now than have thoughts of what might be the reason for your silence.*

*If you have decided we have no future together then please tell me to save me the embarrassment of going to visit your mother on a false pretence. I hope you haven't had a change of feelings. Let me know if you have.*

*Love, Velma*

Jack had to read the letter twice before he could believe what she'd written. How could she believe he'd fallen out of love with her? Didn't she know how deep his feelings were for her?

He frowned. He had written to her every other day ever since he'd left Plymouth. What had happened to the letters? Had he put the wrong address on them? No, he'd sent them to the same place as all the others. He jumped to his feet and hurried over to the barracks.

"Pete, where are you?"

"I'm here," a sleepy voice came from the far bed. "What's the problem? You woke me up yelling like that."

"My letters. What did you do with them?"

"Letters? What letters?"

"My letters to Velma. You said you'd drop them off at the same time you sent yours."

"And I did." Pete sat up and scratched his head. "I -- no wait a minute. Sarge asked me to make the new guy feel useful. You know he's young and a bit homesick, so I promised I'd keep him busy. I've been giving him the letters to drop off at the mail office."

Jack turned away. Pete caught his arm and held him back.

"Let me ask him, Jack. The mood you're in you'll frighten him so much he won't be able to say a word."

The two friends went in search of the new recruit. They soon found him washing down one of the vehicles.

"Hey, Bob. We're looking for some information and wondered if you could help. You know the letters I've been giving you to take to the mail office, did you drop them off?"

Jack moved forward to force the answer from the youngster. Pete nudged him and he stopped.

"The mail office? I thought you meant the post office in town. I had to wait until the next time I got a pass."

"You mean you haven't posted them yet?" Jack couldn't believe his ears. How could anyone be so stupid?

Jack fumed in silence, his fists clenching as Pete retrieved the missing letters and warned young Bob to put them in the camp mail office in future.

"Here you go."

He took the letters from Pete vowing silently to post his own mail from now on. Now he had work to do. He must convince Velma he hadn't fallen out of love with her.

# Chapter Five

*August 1938*

Velma fidgeted as the local train got closer and closer to Hayling Halt. It had been all right while they were on the big train to Portsmouth. She'd made it her job to keep Sam entertained so her sister and George could enjoy the journey. Now they were close to their destination she couldn't cope with a tired four-year-old. All her nerves were on edge as the meeting with Jack's mother loomed.

"Do you think Jack will be there before us, George?"

"Velma, for the umpteenth time, I don't know. He told you he had a weekend pass. They usually start on Friday evening and finish on Sunday evening. If that's the case he won't be here until later tonight."

George had repeated this every time Velma asked about Jack's arrival. She fervently hoped his answer would be different each time. Since receiving the letters from Jack explaining what had happened to the missing ones, which he'd sent as well, she'd become more and more nervous about this visit. She put a lot of importance on Jack being by her side when she met his mother.

The train pulled into the station. Velma and George unloaded the suitcases while Florence helped Sam out of the carriage. Once they were on the platform Velma looked around with trepidation. She didn't think his elderly mother would be here to meet them, but she might think to surprise them. Suddenly, a familiar face loomed out of the crowd. Jack!

Her heart felt as if it would burst from her chest. He moved towards them but something in the way he walked held Velma back. The man was exactly like Jack with some small differences. He walked in a completely different way and his hair parted on the other side. Jack had a soldier's distinct walk. This man moved in a looser fashion. The closer he came, the more she knew this man couldn't be Jack.

"Will," George called out. "Thanks for coming to meet us. This is Florence's sister Velma. She's also Jack's young lady."

Will! Jack's twin. How could she have forgotten they were identical?

"Nice to meet you, Will." Shyness swept over her.

"And nice to meet you too," he replied with a smile. "It's a bit off-putting isn't it?"

"Pardon?"

"Seeing someone with the same face, but it's not the same person. My wife often confuses me with Jack. Luckily, he's away a lot now so it doesn't cause too big a problem."

Velma decided she liked this young man. He might not be her Jack, but he had the same kind and easy going nature. Of course it did help that his face appeared identical to Jack's.

"How's Ma?" George asked as Will led the way off the platform.

"She's well. Excited about seeing you all again. It's this young fellow here she really wants to see." Will ruffled Sam's hair and the youngster grinned up at him. "I hope you don't mind. I borrowed the blacksmith's horse and wagon. I thought Velma might like to see the island in a more leisurely way."

As soon as Sam saw the horse he wanted to give it a carrot. Unfortunately, Will hadn't come prepared for this. He promised the boy he would get a carrot as soon as they reached Grandma's and Sam would be the one to offer it to the mare. They all climbed into the wagon then the horse pulled them on the journey down the leafy lanes.

Velma and Florence sat in the back seat while Sam sat between his father and uncle in the front. They could enjoy the pleasant scenery without having to worry about keeping the boy from getting into mischief.

"I suppose this means Jack isn't here yet," Velma whispered to her sister. "He'd have come to meet us at the station otherwise."

"Velma, stop worrying," Florence scolded. "Ma is lovely. She'll make you feel very welcome."

They lapsed into silence. Velma took note of the fields abundant with their crops and the small cottages lining their route. The island looked beautiful at this time of year. Flowers grew in the cottage gardens filling the air with their scent. The thatch on the cottages and the dusty lanes made everything picturesque and quaint. For the first time Velma wondered where she and Jack would live when they married. Would he still be in the RASC? Would he want to settle on the island? She didn't know if she wanted to move away from her family.

All too soon the wagon drew up outside a neat red brick house at the end of a terrace of similar buildings. Colourful flowers filled the garden and a path went from the gate straight to the front door. Brilliant white net curtains framed the inside of the windows indicating the owner of the house liked things to be clean and neat.

Will and George helped the ladies descend from the wagon and told them they would bring in the bags.

"Ma must be round the back," Will commented. "She doesn't always hear people arriving nowadays. Florence, you and Velma go and find her while George and I get the bags indoors."

The two women each grabbed one of Sam's hands to stop him getting under the men's feet, then Florence led the way round the corner of the house and down a side path.

"Ma, we're here," Florence called as the back of the house came into view.

Velma cringed inside. Time to meet Jack's mother. What would she and Jack do if his mother didn't like her?

*****

Jack climbed down from the third class carriage and hitched his bag up on his shoulder. He wondered if he had time to catch the Hayling Billy over to the island or would he have to run for the ferry?

He entered the booking hall to ask the time of the next train to Hayling Island and bumped into a man turning away from the booking office window.

"Sorry," the man apologised then slapped Jack on the back. "Jack, you old so and so. Come home to see your Ma for the weekend? Do you want a lift over to the island? I've my boat down at the jetty."

"Hello, Jim," Jack greeted his cousin. "That would be good. I'd like to get to Ma's before George and his family arrive."

"You come with me, Jack. I'll make sure you get there first."

Jim led the way down to the shore. Jack slung his bag into the boat, then helped push it off from the beach. Once they were deep enough Jim switched on the motor and they were soon chugging from the mainland to the island.

"So, what's this I hear about you being engaged?"

"Has Will been talking behind my back again?" Jack smiled to show his words were without animosity. "I'm not engaged. I haven't officially asked her yet."

"Who is the luck lady?"

"She's one of Florence's sisters."

Jim set Jack ashore as near to his mother's house as possible. He warned Jack Will had mentioned he had to meet the afternoon train from the mainland. This meant the visitors would already have arrived or they were on their way from the station. It depended on the route Will took and how he transported them.

Jack ran along the short cut he'd often used as a child and arrived breathless at his mother's back garden gate. Would he be in time? He'd just unlatched the gate and walked through when he heard Florence call out.

"Ma, we're here."

*****

Velma took a deep breath and stitched a smile on her face. From the back door of the house an elderly woman emerged. She knew Jack's mother to be only ten years older than her own mother would have been but she seemed so old. Sparse grey hair covered her head and the delicate pinkness of her skin folded into wrinkles of age. When Ma Stanley looked at her, Velma knew what her sister had been trying to tell her. The eyes held a welcome no words could have conveyed. Velma immediately knew this woman would never judge her unfairly. If her son loved her, his mother would also love her.

"Well, I see my two favourite girls have met without bothering to wait for me."

"Jack!" Both women exclaimed and his mother continued. "When did you get here?"

"Just this minute." He gently kissed his mother's wrinkled face then drew Velma to his side and planted a much more robust kiss on her cheek. "Mother, this is Velma, the woman I intend to marry. Velma, this is my lovely mother. The only woman in my heart until you came into my life."

"Oh, you." His mother swatted him with her hand. "You ignore him, Velma. He's got the gift of the gab has this young son of mine. Florence, where's my handsome grandson?"

Florence had been restraining Sam, waiting until Ma met Velma before she released him. Now she let the young scamp go and he made a beeline for his grandmother.

"Gramma. Gramma. Need a carrot."

Jack caught him before he could bowl the old lady over.

"Hey, young man. Haven't you got a hug for your Uncle Jack?"

"Uncle Jack. Need a carrot."

"Why is he saying he needs a carrot?"

"Will promised he could give one to the horse when we got here," Florence explained.

"And as promised here is the carrot and here is Uncle Will." Will appeared from the kitchen waving a large carrot in the air. "Hello, Jack. Sam you come with me. We'll have to be quick. I have to take the horse and wagon back to the blacksmith."

The boy skipped along beside his Uncle Will and the two of them headed for the front of the house. George had followed Will outside and he now greeted his mother.

"Florence, why don't you take Velma up to see her room while I get my two big sons here to help me make a pot of tea?"

Florence pecked Ma on the cheek before taking Velma's arm and leading her into the house. Velma looked back over her shoulder. Could this be a ploy of the older woman's to tell Jack what she really thought of his soon-to-be fiancée?

"Velma, stop worrying. Come on, this is your room." Florence pushed open a door at the front of the house. Her suitcase waited on the bed. "Knowing Ma there'll be fresh water in the ewer so you can wash up. I'll come and get you before I go back down."

Left alone, Velma wanted to cry. All her feelings, doubts and fears crashed together and threatened to overwhelm her. It didn't matter how often Florence told her not to worry, she couldn't help it. She approached the basin with the mirror above and looked at herself. Her lips trembled. At least one of her prayers had been answered. Jack had been there when she met his mother.

She washed quickly and changed into a clean skirt and blouse. As she gave her hair a final pat, Florence knocked on her door. Not wanting to embarrass Jack, Velma valiantly shoved her uneasiness to the back of her mind. Until his mother proved otherwise she'd take the older woman at face value. When the sisters entered the kitchen Ma Stanley sat there on her own.

"The men are playing ball in the garden with young Sam," she told them. "Florence, why don't you go and make sure they don't get up to any mischief. I'm sure Velma won't mind helping me lay the table."

Florence squeezed her sister's shoulder as she passed. Velma's newfound resolve faltered. She had been left alone with Jack's mother.

"That isn't very subtle of me, is it?" A kindly smile crossed Ma's lips and Velma noticed the smile reached her eyes, making the whole face come alive. "Don't you worry, my dear. I'm not going to give you a hard time. My Jack is very precious to me, but then all my children are. If you make him happy, then I'm happy."

"Do you think I make him feel good?" Velma really wanted to know his mother's opinion. Who would know better than the woman who had given birth to him?

"I think you make him very happy, my dear. How do you feel about him?"

"He makes me feel happy, excited and nervous all at once," Velma replied honestly. "I know we haven't known each other very long. It feels we've always been aware the other one waited until the right time. We fit together like two halves of the same whole. Do you understand what I mean?"

"I do indeed, my dear. The same thing happened with Florence and George. I hope you and Jack have the same happiness they found." Jack's mother patted Velma's hand. "I'm so glad we had this little chat. I got the feeling you were nervous about meeting me. You love my Jack as much as he obviously loves you and you'll get no trouble from me. Now let's call the hungry troops in to eat."

While talking they had been laying the table. A bowl of bright green lettuce leaves and startling red tomatoes sat on the snowy white tablecloth surrounded by plates of cold meats, flans and bowls of potatoes. A huge trifle sat on the draining board by the sink, waiting to be plundered and Velma wondered how they were going to get through all this food.

She needn't have worried. Will returned and the three hungry males and the small boy made quick inroads into the main part of the meal. Soon Sam asked for his pudding. By the time they cleared the table the child's head nodded repeatedly toward the table top.

"I think it's time for this young man's bath." Florence pushed her chair back and stood up. "Would you give me a hand please George?"

George picked up his son and followed his wife from the room. Velma took his place at the sink to help with the clearing up. This would be the first chance she'd had to speak with Jack since they'd arrived. Shyness suddenly overcame her.

"How do you feel now you've met Ma?"

"She's lovely, Jack. I can see why you're all so fond of her."

"Well, we think she's something special."

"I thought you said Will got married." Velma wondered why Jack's twin had eaten here instead of at home with his wife. "Won't his wife worry where he's got to?"

"I think Mary had something else on today so she told Will not to rush home. To be honest," Jack glanced quickly over his shoulder. "She's a nice woman, not as good a cook as Ma so Will doesn't mind eating here."

Velma smiled and resolved to ask both Josie and Florence to teach her how to make more interesting recipes than the plain everyday ones she usually did. Maybe when she got to know Jack's mother a bit more the older woman would share some of Jack's favourites. She'd hate to think the other members of Jack's family were criticising her behind her back.

"Ma, Velma and I are going for a walk before it gets too dark." Jack dropped a kiss on his mother's head. "Give you chance to catch up on all the news with George and Florence. We won't be long."

"It's time I left, too," Will stated. "I'll see you tomorrow Jack."

Jack took Velma's hand and led her out the front door and down the path to the gate where they said goodnight to Will. He turned to the right and with a wave of his hand disappeared down the road. Jack turned left and tucked Velma's arm in his. She loved being alone with him. The warm, safe and protected feeling enveloped her again. The weeks between their first meeting and now had forced a small doubt in her mind about her feelings for Jack. Now they were together again, and her doubts disappeared. This man had to be her soul mate and they would be together for the rest of their lives.

They turned off the road into a shady lane. The salty sea air tickled Velma's nose. The short lane ended at the beach. Velma caught her breath as the sun went down over the horizon.

"Jack, this is beautiful."

"Not as beautiful as you." He turned her to face him and pulled her in close. "My lovely Velma. I've missed you so much these last weeks. Have you missed me?"

"Of course I have. My days consisted of going to work, coming home, visiting the family. The only highlights in my empty life were your letters. Did you know you write wonderful letters Jack?"

"When I get your letters I shut my eyes and you're there. Your lovely lavender smell gets trapped in the envelope and you write as you do when you're speaking to me. Velma, let's not wait too long to get married."

A thrill of fear passed through her. She loved Jack but didn't know if she wanted to commit her future to a man who would put his life in danger fighting for his country. What if war happened and he got killed? She'd be left a widow and in her twenties. *At least you'll have known love.* The words were clear in her mind and she remembered Josie telling her about the last war. Her sister had been a teenager and she'd seen the broken men coming home to their wives, and the women whose husbands didn't come home. Velma had asked if the women regretted getting married only to lose their loved ones. Josie's reply had been the women were glad to have had even that short time with their men.

*She's right. Even if Jack gets killed, we'll have some time together.*

"Velma, are you listening to me?" Jack interrupted her thoughts.

"Sorry, I was daydreaming."

"About me I hope." He smiled down at her. "Don't worry, my love, I'm not rushing you into an immediate marriage. I want to know if you'll marry me next year. August or September perhaps. What do you say?"

"I'd love to marry you, Jack, and next year sounds perfect. It gives my sisters time to fuss over the arrangements. They wouldn't think it a proper marriage if we didn't do the whole white wedding thing."

Jack pulled up one leg of his army issue trousers and knelt down on the sand. Velma stood in stunned silence as he took her hand in both of his. She looked down into his deep brown eyes and waited breathlessly for what she hoped he would say.

"Velma Field. I want you to be the mother of my children and my companion for the rest of our lives. Will you do me the honour of becoming my wife?"

"Yes." Velma's answer barely disturbed the silence on the beach.

"Pardon?"

"Yes, Jack, yes. I'd love to marry you." The words came out breathlessly. Velma found it hard to believe Jack had proposed in the traditional way.

With a whoop of joy Jack sprang to his feet and lifted Velma off the ground. He swung her round and round in a circle until she begged him to stop. When he did at last set her back on the ground he took a step back and fumbled in his pocket.

"You said yes so I guess you'd better have this."

He held a small velvet box in the palm of his hand. Velma held her breath as he lifted the lid and plucked a ring from the plush cream interior. Jack pushed the box back into his pocket, lifted her left hand to his lips and kissed her ring finger. Carefully, he slid the ring onto her finger, then pulled her close.

Velma melted into his arms as he pulled her closer and his lips met hers. She twined her arms around his neck as she lost herself in his kiss. Jack stroked her back, and down her arm. As his hand passed her breast it brushed against her nipple. An excited tremor passed through Velma, followed by flush of embarrassment.

The hand returned and completely covered the breast, squeezing gently, then one finger reached up and traced a line down the bare skin above the top of the neckline. His hand moved to the buttons of her dress and she sensed rather than felt him undo them one at a time in a slow, leisurely pace. The front of the garment parted and cool air passed over her skin.

Jack stopped and drew back slightly. She smiled at him, aware of him asking silently for permission to go a step further. She pulled him closer and took his hand to place it on her breast outside of her bra. For a second, she glanced down. The whiteness of her skin and bra showed starkly against the dark suntan of his hand. Again, the thrill of this new experience ran through her.

Gently Jack stroked her breast through the lacy material. He reached inside the cup and lifted her breast free of its restraint. Velma gasped as he stroked her skin and tweaked her nipple. Jack stopped and looked at her again, before carrying on with his caress. Once more his lips found hers then he ducked his head and kissed her on the bare white skin below her neck. His head dipped. As his lips and tongue plucked and licked the bud of her nipple, she gasped again. Her breast rose eagerly for this new source of excitement.

Velma had never experienced emotions like this before. Her love for Jack made her want to give in to his needs, but her upbringing told her to push him away. Her breasts strained for his touch. Between her thighs the most delicious, warm, moist feeling overcame her. She knew she had lost control and love had won. It didn't matter, she no longer cared.

Jack's hand covered her breast again as he popped it back into her bra. Her eyes flew open. One after the other he did up her buttons.

"I think we'd better stop now, Velma." Pent up emotion roughened his voice. "If we don't I might not be able to control myself."

Disappointment swept through her. She knew he had been right. She loved him and would allow him more licence with her body than she had with any other man. Velma still wanted to be a virgin on her wedding night. The thought of marrying this man next year and allowing him to take her completely almost made her throw herself at him. She forced herself under control and helped him rearrange her clothing.

For the first time she looked at the ring on her finger. Three small diamonds were held in the curves of a wavy strip of white gold, one in the depth of each wave. The gems winked in the last light of the sun and the tears prick Velma's eyes.

"Do you like it?"

"Jack, it's beautiful."

She flung her arms around him and kissed him once more.

When they surfaced the sun had dropped behind the horizon, but its orange red glow still lit up the sky. Hand in hand they walked down to the edge of the water to watch the glorious sight gradually darken as the night claimed the land and sea.

# Chapter Six

"So, do we tell the family now or do we wait?" Jack squeezed her hand as they walked back to his mother's house.

"I think we should tell Florence, George and your mother," Velma said thoughtfully. "It might be the only chance we get to tell your mother when both of us are there. We'll swear the other two to silence until I can get my family together and tell them all at once. They get very irritated if they think one sister knows something before the others."

Jack squeezed her hand and she smiled up at him. To be with him and know he would be her husband filled her with a warm glow inside.

"There you are. We thought you two had got lost." Velma blushed, but Florence carried on. "We're just going to have a cup of cocoa before we go to bed. It's been a long day with all this travelling."

A few minutes later they sat around the table with mugs of cocoa in front of them. Velma hid her hand under the overhang of the tablecloth. She glanced over at Jack and nodded.

"While we're all here, Velma and I have something to tell you."

Florence and Ma smiled happily when Velma blushed again. George looked round with a blank face. Velma knew the poor man didn't have a clue what his brother had to say.

"Velma has done me the honour of agreeing to be my wife." The words tumbled out and Velma wondered if it was due to nervousness.

Florence rushed around the table.

"I'm so happy for you, Velma. I knew you two were made for each other the moment I saw you together in my kitchen."

"Welcome to our family, my dear. Forgive me for not getting up; it's the problem with old bones." Ma smiled at her. "Come and give me a hug both of you."

Jack enfolded both his mother and his fiancée in his arms. He smiled at Velma over the top of his mother's head, love shining from his eyes. When they'd settled down again and the women had admired the engagement ring, Florence questioned the couple.

"When are you thinking of tying the knot? Not too soon I hope, Velma. You know how the family is. They'll want to make sure everything's done properly."

"We were thinking of August or September next year. It gives us time to plan the wedding and what happens next. I'm not even sure where Jack wants to live."

"I'll be away a lot with the RASC to begin with so it's probably best if you stay in Plymouth. You'll have your family near you so you won't be lonely."

"But I hope you'll come and visit me when you can, Velma," Ma interjected.

*****

Jack sat listening to the women planning his future. He didn't mind. He wanted Velma to have the wedding of her dreams. He really thought she should live in Plymouth. Although he hadn't mentioned the prospect of war, it lurked in his mind and he didn't want Velma to be with strangers if the government declared war on Germany.

He watched his mother join in the conversation and a frown crossed his brow. They would presumably marry in Plymouth. Would this mean his beloved Ma wouldn't be able to attend? He'd have to think of a way to solve this as his mother and Velma were the most important people in his life.

The following day passed quickly. Next morning Jack took his brand new fiancée to visit the immediate family who still lived on the island. By the time they returned to Ma's for lunch, poor Velma looked shell shocked.

"We don't have any more to visit do we?"

"No, my love," he told her. "There are more who don't live nearby. One of my brothers lives in Argentina so I doubt if you'll ever meet him."

"I don't mean to be rude, but thank goodness we've finished. It's exhausting being introduced to people and knowing they're watching to see if you're good enough for their little brother."

Velma suddenly broke into peals of laughter and Jack looked at her with surprise.

"Sorry." She choked down the giggles. "That's exactly what happened with you and my family. Shame we're not only children, it would make life a lot easier."

"But we'd miss out on a lot more excitement and I expect it would be a bit boring too."

Lunch over, Jack and George got on with some jobs Ma wanted done and later they all went for a walk along the beach. Sam thoroughly enjoyed rushing at the tiny waves that broke on the sand and then running away before they could touch him. Eventually, George took off his shoes and socks and rolled up his trousers. He did the same for his son and the two of them went paddling at the edge of the sea. Jack watched his brother thinking how some day he might be doing that with his and Velma's son. A warm feeling grew inside of him as he thought of the children they might have.

The remaining time flew by and all too soon Jack said goodbye to Velma and his brother's family. They had a lot further to travel than he did so their train left an hour before his. The others had already loaded the suitcases and themselves onto the carriage. Jack intended to hold Velma in his arms as long as possible. He wanted to remember the touch and smell of her when he lay in his lonely bed in the Aldershot barracks.

"You'll write and let me know how your family takes the news won't you?"

"Of course I will, Jack. Don't worry, they'll be thrilled. Is it all right if I find out some available dates at the church?"

"You do whatever you need to do, my love. Once you let me know the possibilities I'll check and see when I can have leave. Plus, I have to get permission to marry."

He could tell by the look on her face she'd forgotten someone in the armed forces needed permission.

"Don't worry. My captain is an understanding man. Plus we're not asking to rush out and get married next week. As long as we have several date options, he should be very accommodating."

The guard blew his whistle and Jack kissed her one last time, then helped her onto the train and slammed the carriage door behind her. She pulled down the window and reached out. Catching her hand in his, he walked beside the carriage as the train slowly moved. Eventually, he ran out of platform and had to let go. He remained standing there until the last glimpse of the white hand waving goodbye had disappeared round the corner of the track.

*****

Velma woke up in her own bed on Monday morning and wondered if she'd dreamed the previous few days. She and Jack had had such a short time together. Had it all occurred in her imagination? She looked at the ring hanging round her neck on a chain Ma had given her. She smiled. It had definitely happened.

She wriggled happily. She and Jack were getting married. Florence had been sworn to secrecy. No one could know until the weekend family get together next Sunday. George didn't see the need to keep it quiet. Florence spoke to him and he promised he wouldn't mention it. They had considered telling Josie. Her older sister hated trouble and she would have wanted to tell everyone immediately, knowing the others would be down on her like a ton of bricks if she'd known and not told them.

The alarm went off and Velma shoved back the covers and jumped out of bed. Minutes later she clattered down the stairs and into the kitchen.

"Morning, Josie."

Her sister busily made a pot of tea and toasted the bread for breakfast.

"You seem happy. It must be the break and seeing Jack again."

"I had a lovely time. I don't know why I got so worried about meeting his mother. Ma's a lovely lady and she made me feel very welcome. I don't think I want any breakfast. I'll just grab some toast and eat it as I walk to work."

"You'll do no such thing. Sit down and eat properly. Whatever will people think if they see you walking along eating your breakfast?"

Velma gave in gracefully. She knew of no way to sway Josie's mind when it came to keeping up appearances. Eventually, she escaped and strolled into the town, daydreaming about her future with Jack. Her steps slowed until Gladdie came rushing up behind her.

"Why are you so slow, Velma? If you don't hurry we'll be late. How did you enjoy your weekend?"

Velma sped up to keep pace with Gladdie and minutes later they were in the staff cloakroom putting on their overalls. She still hadn't answered Gladdie's question. What should she tell her best friend? Should she tell Gladdie, or wait until she'd told the family? Gladdie had been with her all through school and they'd joined the store on the same day. Her friend had never broken her confidence before so she would certainly keep Velma's secret. A saying of Florence's came to mind. *You can choose your friends but not your relatives.* Much as she loved her family they could be a bit silly and proprietary at times. If Velma didn't say anything to Gladdie her friend would be hurt she hadn't trusted her to keep the secret.

"Gladdie, what are you doing lunchtime? I need to talk to you about something private."

Her friend looked at her with a solemn expression on her face and nodded. Velma wondered what had gone through the other woman's mind.

"Meet me in here in the cloakroom and we'll go for a cup of tea. Come on, or we'll be late."

Velma frowned as she followed her friend down the stairs. Usually Gladdie started interrogating her for a hint of what she wanted to discuss. Did Gladdie know her secret? Of course not. Perhaps she'd guessed.

At lunchtime the two friends ate their packed lunches in the staff cloakroom then covered their overalls with cardigans and clattered down the stairs. By the time they sat with pot of tea between them in a nearby café they only had half an hour left of their lunch break.

"Tell me, what's so secret?"

"You know, don't you?"

"Velma, if you need my help you've got to know I'll be there for you, no matter how bad it is. Just tell me what's wrong."

*Oh heavens. She thinks I'm pregnant.*

"Gladdie, Jack asked me to marry him. We've decided on August or September next year. You have to keep it secret for a few days though."

"Oh, Velma, I'm so pleased." The worried expression left Gladdie's face and she positively beamed at Velma. "You must be so happy."

"You thought Jack had got me..." Velma glanced around to make sure no one could overhear them. She lowered her voice to a whisper. "...pregnant, didn't you?"

"Well, yes. I couldn't think of any other reason why you wanted to tell me something private. Why don't you want anyone to know?"

"It's only until the weekend. You know what my sisters are like. If they think one of them knows before the other they'll get really mad." She allowed her friend to see her concern. The relief at confiding in Gladdie made her feel a lot better. "Poor Florence is worried sick. She thinks everyone will turn on her as it will be obvious she knows. We needed to tell Jack's mum so it couldn't be helped. You will keep it quiet won't you, until I've told the rest of the family?"

"Have you told Josie?"

"No." Velma leaned back in her chair. "Josie would be worse than Florence. She'd imagine all sorts of things the sisters would say or do. At least I have someone to discuss it with now." She grinned at Gladdie. "I'm assuming you will. I suppose I should ask. You will be my bridesmaid won't you? My only bridesmaid."

Gladdie let out a squeal and Velma quickly hushed her.

"Of course I will, Velma. Why the only one?"

"I've got far too many nieces and nephews. This way I get who I want to attend me. Would you like to see my ring?"

Gladdie gave a suitable gasp as she inspected the diamonds. They spent the rest of the time discussing wedding clothes and how they needed to start visiting the bridal departments of the big stores to see the different styles of wedding dress. Gladdie also mentioned present lists, seating plans and lists of people to invite. Velma's heart sank. She hadn't imagined there would be so much work involved in marrying the man she loved.

"Don't worry, Velma. Your sisters will probably take over and do all those things. You won't have to worry about anything. Just concentrate on being beautiful for your man." Her friend grinned. "Of course inviting suitable single gentlemen for your best friend's entertainment is one thing you need to do."

The days sped towards the weekend. Velma's apprehension grew when she thought about facing the family with her news. She knew they liked Jack. Would they want him as part of the family?

Josie had planned the usual tea and she got quite cross when Velma dropped a plate of bread and butter.

"Whatever's the matter with you? You're all fingers and thumbs. Anyone would think you've got something on your mind."

"Don't be silly, Josie, I'm just tired. I didn't sleep well last night."

She'd told the truth. She imagined all sorts of responses when she'd announced her wedding plans, so much so that sleep eluded her for most of the night.

Velma had just finished clearing up the mess she'd made when Enid and her husband arrived, closely followed by the other sisters. A visibly nervous Florence and her family were last. George headed straight for the men and Velma smiled. The poor man considered this to be women's business and wanted no part of it.

When everyone had their plates of cake and cups of tea Velma took a deep breath and tapped the side of her cup with her teaspoon.

"I have something I'd like to tell everyone." Her voice grew stronger as she spoke. "Last weekend Jack asked me to marry him and I said yes."

As one, the heads of the sisters turned to look at Florence who tried to sink down into the depths of her chair.

"You are not to blame Florence for keeping this a secret. We asked her not to tell until you were all here. She wouldn't have known anything about it. When we told Jack's mother Florence and George were there. Florence didn't want to keep it from you." The sisters accepted this. They turned their head towards Josie and Velma hurried on. "And Josie didn't know a thing about it so don't you start accusing her."

Now the news had been digested, the sisters flung questions at her. When were they intending to get married? Where? Would Jack's family attend?

"I don't think you should rush into this." Enid sat ramrod straight as she made this declaration.

Velma knew Enid would be the one to object. Her eldest sister had considered herself the matriarch of the family even when their Mother still lived.

"You need to get to know him better before you take such a big step." Enid continued. "You know very little about the sort of person he is."

"Enid, he's George's brother." Florence couldn't hide her anger. Velma watched the expressions of amazement, irritation and stubbornness flit across Enid's face. "If you're saying Jack is not good enough for Velma, it's like saying George's family isn't good enough for our family."

"I said nothing of the sort, Florence. You're overreacting."

"Then what is your objection?" Florence demanded.

"All I'm saying is we shouldn't give our permission for Velma to marry Jack until she gets to know him better."

"I beg your pardon?" Velma couldn't believe she'd heard right. "It's not up to you, Enid. I am over twenty-one and I don't need your permission."

"Why don't we all have a nice cup of tea?" Josie tried to calm the charged tension in the room.

"That's an excellent idea, Josie." Velma smiled at her sister to show her thanks for Josie's attempt to regain the peace. "But first please know that I am telling you I am getting married, not asking your permission. This part of the conversation is now over."

She ignored the gasps of outrage from the assembled women and turned and helped Josie pour the tea into the cups, despite her shaking hands.

"It will be white wedding, won't it? And I suppose he will eventually buy you a ring."

Velma hid a grin at Enid's sharply voiced question. Her eldest sister didn't like to be opposed in anything. Slowly, Velma withdrew the ring from its hiding place and placed it on her finger. Her sisters crowded round. They all looked at Enid, waiting for her to signal her approval.

"Very nice." Enid sniffed.

"To answer your question, Enid. Yes it will be a white wedding. I should tell you now there will only be one attendant. My friend Gladdie."

This caused another uproar in the room. Each sister thought her child would make the best bridesmaid or pageboy. Tears threatened to overflow Velma's eyes. She gritted her teeth, determined to stand her ground.

"Enough." To her surprise her brother John had entered the room.

"I've been standing here listening to you squabble about what should be a happy occasion. It should follow Velma and Jack's wishes not yours. I think she's being very sensible. She can't have all the nieces and nephews so rather than upset some of you she's chosen the closest thing to family. Her best friend." He turned to face Velma. "You go for it, love. Don't let this lot put you off doing what your heart tells you is right."

Having delivered his words of wisdom, John rejoined the men in the other room. All of them looked at him with admiration. Velma knew none of them would have dared contradict their wives, but a brother had a special standing with the harem.

# Chapter Seven

*April 1939*

Velma and Gladdie carried their suitcases down the road to Ma Stanley's house.

"Are you sure Jack's mother won't mind me turning up like this?"

"Don't be silly, Gladdie. Of course she won't mind. She's always telling me to bring some friends with me. I think she feels she'll get to know me better if she sees the people I meet every day."

Velma spoke the truth. She'd been to visit Ma two or three times, once without Jack and the older woman had made her feel extremely welcome and encouraged her to bring a friend with her.

"And do you have a young man?" Ma wanted to know.

"No, I haven't been as lucky as Velma," Gladdie confessed. "I'm still looking though."

All three women laughed.

"I promise I'll keep a watch for any men I think might be suitable for you," Ma stated.

Later in the evening the two friends walked along the beach to watch the sun set.

"It's beautiful here," Gladdie sighed. "Will you and Jack live here when you're married?"

"Not at first. Jack says it's best if I stay in Plymouth until we see what's happening with Germany. I suppose we might end up living here. We'll see what happens."

"You don't sound very enthusiastic." Gladdie stopped and looked directly at Velma. "What if Jack leaves the services and gets a job on the island?"

"There aren't any jobs on the island, that's why he joined up in the first place."

"Don't try and fool me, Velma Field. You know what I mean and you're skirting round the subject. He could always work in Portsmouth or Havant. It's so easy to get to and from the island."

"I'm not sure how I feel Gladdie. I don't want to leave Plymouth and all my friends and family. If Jack really wants to live here, I will. I love him so much I'll go anywhere with him. I'm hoping he'd rather stay in Plymouth."

"I wouldn't worry about it. It'll all sort itself out and if you do have to live on Hayling Island, I'll have somewhere to take my holidays won't I?"

The two friends laughed and arm in arm carried on along the beach.

*****

*September 1939*

*"I am speaking to you from the Cabinet Room at 10 Downing Street.*

*"This morning the British Ambassador in Berlin handed the German Government a final note stating that unless we heard from them by 11.00 a.m. that they were prepared at once to withdraw their troops from Poland, a state of war would exist between us.*

*"I have to tell you that no such undertaking has been received and that consequently this country is at war with Germany..."*

Velma, Josie and Tom listened in appalled silence as Neville Chamberlain continued to read the Declaration of War.

*Jack had been right. War is here and now he'll have to go where the fighting is.* Velma knew her thoughts were selfish. She could only think of Jack and how this horrible declaration would affect their relationship.

"Well, I know one thing," she stated defiantly. "That rotten Hitler is not going to ruin my wedding. I won't let him."

"Don't be silly, Velma," Josie told her. "They've only announced the Declaration today. It will take time to mobilise the army and navy. Your wedding's a few weeks away. Everything will be all right."

Later that night, Velma lay in bed fervently hoping the war wouldn't interfere with her future. The past year had been wonderful. She and Jack had spent several weekends together in Plymouth and on Hayling Island. They'd walked along the beach on the island, visited the Lido in Plymouth and grown so close they really were two halves of one whole.

She sighed and punched the pillow, trying to get comfortable enough to forget the worries about the war. It had been nearly two months since the last time she had seen Jack. He had saved his leave for the honeymoon. Would they be able to have a honeymoon now?

Last time they'd been together, Jack had looked tired. They'd been at his mother's house and he'd arrived late in the evening. Ma had tactfully gone to bed early so they could sit and talk.

"I think this will be the last time I can get away for a while. I have to make sure I've got some leave saved so we can spend a bit of time together after the wedding."

Velma snuggled in to his arms and raised her face for a kiss.

"Is there anything I need to do for the wedding?"

"I don't think so. My sisters have it all under control," Velma replied. "Have you worked out how to get Ma to Plymouth yet?"

"Will and Mary are going to bring her down two days before so she has time to get over the journey. Florence said Ma can stay at her house."

"Really! She hasn't told me." Velma frowned wondering why her sister had kept it a secret.

"I think she didn't want to disappoint you. Ma's still not sure she'll be able to make the journey. I think she'll wait until a few days before she has to travel, then she'll make her decision whether or not to come."

"I hope she can. It won't be the same without her." The news clouded Velma's happiness for a moment, but she couldn't stay down for long. Not when Jack held her in his arms. "Where are we going for our honeymoon, Jack?"

"It's a secret." Humour lit Jack's eyes and Velma rose to the challenge.

"Give me a clue."

"It's somewhere quiet where we can take things easy." Jack grinned. "It's also near to a town so we can go out to the movies or for a meal. I'm not going to tell you any more than that."

"I won't ask any more. I love surprises and don't want to spoil this one." Velma knew didn't really matter where they went. Anywhere they were together was the right place.

Jack stroked the side of her face. Velma leaned her cheek into his touch. She found it amazing they'd only known each other for just over a year. She couldn't imagine her life without Jack.

The weekend passed too quickly then Jack put Velma on the train back to Plymouth.

"Goodbye, my love. I'll see you a few days before our wedding."

Velma could still feel the tingle of Jack's final kiss as the train pulled away from the platform.

*****

"Oh, Velma, you're so beautiful." Josie had tears in her eyes.

Velma faced the mirror. The reflection seemed like a different person. She could never be this beautiful. Her skin returned the glow of the ivory satin empire line dress. A sparkling tiara peeped through her shining dark hair while the lace veil she dropped over her face, made her appear mysterious and unobtainable.

"You don't think it's too much, do you?"

"Not a bit," Josie replied. "Brides are supposed to look wonderful on their wedding day. The veil adds a touch of mystery."

"I hope Jack likes it. Oh Josie, I can hardly believe it." Velma did a little hop of excitement. "This time next week I'll be Mrs. Jack Stanley instead of plain old Velma Field."

"Let's get you out of that dress and hang it up."

Velma could see tears in Josie's eyes as her sister bent her head and moved round to undo the fastenings at the back of the dress. Josie had been like a mother to her. The other sisters had helped, but Josie and her husband had put aside their own desire for children in order to bring up the little girls who needed someone to love and care for them. As Josie turned from hanging up the wedding dress Velma flung her arms around her.

"Thank you, Josie. Thank you for everything."

"Silly girl." Tears still sparkled in Josie's eyes as she held Velma at arms length for a few moments before hugging her tight again. "I haven't done anything."

A knock at the front door interrupted the tender moment. Josie muttered to herself. "Now who could that be? You get yourself presentable Velma and come downstairs. No doubt it's one of the sisters come to chat about the wedding."

Velma pulled a cotton dress down over her head. As she tidied her hair she heard a male voice downstairs. Could that be one of her brothers-in-law? Or had her poor brother been dragged on a visit by his wife. She hurried down to help Josie make the tea.

Her sister stood at the kitchen sink a worried expression on her face.

"What's the matter, Josie? Who knocked on the door?"

"Velma. It's Jack. He's in the living room. You'd better go and see him."

Velma didn't hear past the fact Jack had appeared in the living room. Her feet barely touched the floor as she ran out of the kitchen.

"Jack." She burst into the room to find him standing before the empty fireplace. He turned slowly to face her. The sad and apprehensive expression on his face halted her rush to his side.

"What's the matter, Jack? What's happened?"

He shouldn't have arrived for the wedding until Thursday. She'd assumed he'd got away a few days early, but a horrible suspicion stirred inside her. The look on his face told her something terrible had happened. Cold fear crept through her. His expression warned his next words could affect their whole future.

"Velma I..." Jack stopped and took her hands in his. "Sweetheart, I don't know how to tell you this. I can't marry you on Saturday."

# Chapter Eight

Velma's world collapsed around her. She'd trusted Jack implicitly. She'd told him her deepest secrets. She'd let him have far more liberty with her body than she'd ever allowed any other man or boy. Now he'd had second thoughts. A suspicion grew in her mind.

"Did you tell Josie this? Is that why she's looking so upset? You could at least have told me you were jilting me before you spoke to her."

"Jilting you? Who said anything about jilting you?"

"You're not leaving me at the altar? Then why are you calling off the wedding?" Confusion overwhelmed her. His words were contradictory.

"Come and sit down. Let me explain."

Velma reluctantly allowed herself to be drawn down onto the settee. Jack kept hold of her hand, his thumb caressing her palm as he looked deep into her eyes. Despite her anger she couldn't help feeling a thrill of excitement at his touch.

"This had better be good," she warned him.

"First of all, you have to believe I love you, Velma. My heart is yours and will always be yours." He paused, took a deep breath and rushed on, his gaze still capturing hers. "You know England declared war on Germany last week? We were put on alert. The captain assured me I'd still be able to get married as planned, although the honeymoon would have to wait."

"Oh, Jack."

"Hush, I haven't finished." He placed a finger on her lips. "The captain got it wrong. We're shipping out at the end of the week. By the time our wedding day arrives I won't be here."

Velma's heart plummeted. Sadness welled up inside of her. Her dreams of a white wedding were at the best postponed, at the worst completely ended. Fear for Jack overwhelmed her disappointment. He would be fighting for his country and he might get hurt. Or worse still, he could be killed. Tears sprang to her eyes.

"I understand, Jack. We'll have to wait until..."

"No, Velma. That's not it. We can still get married, but not the big wedding we've planned. I've arranged it all at the registry office in Aldershot." He pulled a piece of paper from his uniform pocket. "See. I've got a special license. Thing is you'll have to come with me now -- today. What do you say? Will you still marry me? Without the church and family there?"

"Of course I will." Velma didn't hesitate. "A big white wedding with both of our families would have been nice. The most important thing is you and me Jack. I wouldn't feel you were properly prepared to face the enemy if we weren't married. What do I need to do?"

*****

Jack pulled her into a hug then kissed her soundly. He drew back slightly and stroked the side of her face. Love shone from his eyes and she hoped her own showed him how much she cared.

"Velma, I love you so much." He took her hands from her lap and held them tightly between his own. "Pack the outfit you want to be married in and be ready to leave as soon as possible. There's a train at midnight. We have to be on it. I've got to get back to the barracks by tomorrow midday and we can get married the next day."

"Thursday the fourteenth. It's only two days before we were supposed to have the big do. How long do you think we'll have before you go?" Velma forced her nerves and stomach flutters to be still. If the wedding was to take place, the time had come to be practical.

"One night. Maybe two. I won't know until I get back and see what's happened. I'm lucky my captain let me come and get you before we leave."

"Let's go and tell Josie what's going on."

Jack stood and pulled Velma up and into his arms. He held her close and kissed the tip of her nose.

"I love you so much, Velma. We'll have a wonderful life together."

Still holding hands, they went to the kitchen to tell Josie about the change in plans. Velma's heart plummeted. Her eldest sister Enid sat at the kitchen table.

"Jack. What are you doing here young man? You're not supposed to arrive until later this week. Why aren't you training to protect your country?" Enid's words were snapped out in a regimented fashion. Velma had the urge to jump to attention and salute.

"I'm glad you're here, Enid. We have some news about the wedding. If you hear it at the same time as Josie you won't be able to blame her will you?"

The older woman spluttered in indignation. Behind her Josie flapped her hands in agitation.

"There isn't going to be a wedding." Velma waited while both the other women gasped. She opened her mouth to continue before Enid could begin to attack Jack.

"I knew it," Josie spoke in a nervous voice. "I knew something had happened as soon as Jack appeared on the doorstep."

"Now look here young man." Enid used her 'no nonsense' voice. "If you think you are going to jilt Velma, then think again. You've swept her off her feet and talked her into marrying you. It's too late now to get cold feet. The wedding is all arranged."

"Enid, for once in your life be quiet and listen." Velma stood in front of Jack with hands on her hips. "There is not going to be a white wedding. Jack won't be here. His company is going overseas by the end of the week. I'm going to Aldershot with him tonight and we'll be married in a registry office on Thursday."

"You'll do no such thing." Enid's chest heaved and the irritated look on her face changed to one of horror. "The shame of it. People will think you have to get married. No, we'll postpone the wedding. You can get married when Jack comes home on leave."

The older woman picked up her handbag and rose from her chair. She headed for the door but stopped as Velma spoke quietly.

"Enid. I'll see you when I get back from Aldershot."

With an outraged expression, Enid left. Josie busied herself at the sink and Velma went and put her arms around her sister's shoulders.

"Don't worry, Josie. She can't blame you. If the other sisters say anything, tell them Enid tried to stop me, too, and she didn't have any luck."

Josie turned and tears sparkled in her sister's eyes.

"Oh don't, Josie. Please don't cry. Be happy for me. I don't really care about the white wedding. I just want us to be married before Jack goes away."

Her sister took a handkerchief from her pocket and blew her nose.

"This isn't getting us anywhere." Josie bravely tried to smile. "What time is your train?"

"The midnight one." Jack spoke for the first time since they'd entered the kitchen. "Josie, I'm sorry about all this. It can't be helped."

"We'd better get on with things hadn't we? Velma, I'll help you pack. Jack, you'd better pop round to George and Florence and tell them what's happening. George will be able to let your family know. Go on. Off you go."

Velma laughed as Jack allowed himself to be shooed out the door. Then she followed Josie up the stairs to her bedroom.

"Be honest with me, Velma. Are you very disappointed you won't be wearing this lovely dress?" Josie ran her fingers gently down the satin of the skirt. "You could wait you know. Jack will probably be home on leave in a few months."

"Josie, please don't be cross with me. This is what Jack and I want. Yes, it would have been lovely to get married in church with all the family around us, but it's not possible." Determined to have her own way, Velma looked her sister in the eye. "I won't have Jack going off to war before we get married. This is the only way we can become husband and wife. You do understand don't you?"

"Of course I do." Josie hugged her, then carried on briskly. "Now why don't you wear your going away suit to get married in?"

*****

"Jack, what are you doing here?" He hadn't intended to frighten

54

Florence when he walked into the kitchen. His sister-in-law looked startled when she saw him. "I didn't expect you until Thursday. I haven't got your room ready yet."

"Change of plans, Florence. Where's George?"

"He's out in the garden with Sam. Jack, is there anything wrong?"

"No, at least I hope you won't think it's wrong. Could you call George in please? I need to speak to you both."

Florence hurried out to the garden and returned in moments with her husband and son.

"Uncle Jack." Sam rushed over and tried to climb up Jack's leg. Jack immediately reached down and picked him up, holding him high in the air.

"Hello Sam, you're getting bigger each time I see you."

Florence had been busy at the stove. As Jack put Sam down, she called her son to her. "Now Sam, you take this cup of milk and sit there with your toys. Mummy, Daddy and Uncle Jack have grown up things to talk about." Sam carefully carried his cup to where his toys cluttered the floor and sat down with his back against the sofa. "Good boy."

"What's up, Jack?" George asked as Florence placed cups of tea on the table and they all sat down. "Why are you here so early?"

Jack quietly explained about his company going overseas and how all leave had been cancelled.

"But the wedding! What about the wedding?" Florence's voice verged on hysteria. "Everything's arranged."

"I'm sorry, Florence, it will have to be cancelled. Velma's coming to Aldershot with me. We're going to be married in the registry office on Thursday."

Florence gasped and the colour drained from her face. Her hand flew to her heart and George reached across, picked up her cup of tea and brought it to her lips.

"Calm down, Florence. What will be, will be."

"But Enid! What will she say when she finds out?"

"You all take far too much notice of Enid." Jack couldn't help the irritation in his voice. "It's got nothing to do with her. She already knows."

"She does?" Surprise sprang into her expression. "How did she take it?"

"Enid declared people would think we had to get married. Velma put her in her place though."

"*Velma* did?"

"You know, Florence, none of you give Velma the respect she deserves. You all think of her as the baby of the family and don't realise she's grown up and has a mind of her own. Velma feels as I do." For a moment irritation took over Jack's usually calm manner. "We want to get married before I go overseas. This is the only way we can do that, so it doesn't matter what the family say, Velma's coming to Aldershot with me."

George smiled and patted his wife's hand. "When are you leaving?"

"We're catching the midnight train. Josie's helping Velma pack."

"Good luck over there, brother." George held out his hand. "I'll be following you soon. Florence will keep an eye on Velma. Not that she needs it of course. Tell her Florence is here for her if she needs any help."

"Thanks, George." Jack shook his brother's hand. "I've a favour to ask you. Could you let Ma know? I haven't got time to go home and explain things, but I don't want her to think I got married behind her back."

"Leave it with me. When do you have to be back at Velma's? Do you have time for a quick meal?"

"I should really get back there before it gets dark. I do have time for a cup of tea and something light. I hope it's not too much trouble, Florence?"

"Of course not." She hurried to the pantry to prepare some food.

*****

Velma took Josie's advice. She would wear her 'going away' suit for her wedding. She considered it a smart and dressy outfit. Their wedding wouldn't appear to be a last minute rush if she wore this. Her battered suitcase would have to do to hold the rest of her clothes. She'd only be gone a few days so she didn't need much.

"A few days!" Horror at the thought of Mrs. Harris' reaction rushed through Velma. "Josie, what am I going to do about work?"

"They'll understand." Josie put an arm around her sister's shoulders. "Don't worry. Leave it with me. I'll go and explain it all to your supervisor. You just concentrate on you and Jack."

"Josie, have I ever told you you're the best sister in the entire world?" Velma threw her arms around the older woman and hugged her. "You always had time for me as a child and I feel I can tell you anything. You understand me better than any of the others, with the possible exception of Florence."

Josie hugged her back then moved away and lifted the corner of her apron to wipe the tear from her eye.

"You'd better make sure you've got everything, then bring your case downstairs. I'll put the kettle on and get the tea."

Josie left the room and Velma checked she had all she might need. Instead of taking her case down, she sat on the bed and looked around the room. It had been hers for as long as she could remember. The older sisters had brought up the younger children when it became obvious their mother couldn't take care of them. Josie had given up a lot for her younger siblings and Velma hoped her sister knew how much she appreciated the love and care given to her.

*Next time I sleep in this room I'll be a married woman.*

She found the thought daunting. The original intention had been for Velma to stay with Josie until Jack could get accommodation in Aldershot for them. Now it made more sense for Velma to stay her with her family until it became clear how the war would affect everything.

A little bit of sadness shadowed her happiness, before thoughts of Jack and their future together brought her excitement bubbling up again. Velma jumped off the bed with a little hop. She collected the case and went downstairs to wait for the man who would soon be her husband.

*****

"Where is he?" Velma paced up and down the kitchen.

"He'll be here," Josie consoled her. "Now, are you sure you have everything?"

"Yes. I've gone over everything twice and I'm sure I've got all I need."

"Are you going to be warm enough in that suit? It's colder in Hampshire. You don't want to get married with your nose blue from the cold."

"She won't have to."

Velma spun round to see Enid standing in the doorway.

*I really wish she'd knock instead of just walking in.* Velma couldn't help the irritated feeling she had for this overbearing elder sister.

"Hello, Enid." Velma tried to sound warm, but warily waited for Enid to continue. What did her older sister mean?

"Velma, I've thought about what you said. I don't agree with the way you're getting married. You're quite right about being old enough to make up your own mind. At your age I had been married a few years and given birth to two children. If this is the way you and Jack want to get married, then at least I can help. You don't want people to think it's some hole-in-the-corner affair." Enid offered a bag to Velma.

Wondering what on earth Enid could be giving her, Velma peeped inside the bag.

"But -- but this is your fur coat, Enid." She couldn't believe her eyes. Enid never let anyone borrow her precious coat.

"You take good care of it. I want it back in the same condition as I gave it to you." Enid straightened her shoulders and gave a little huff. "At least now people won't think you're having a 'quickie' marriage."

Josie stood behind Enid and Velma nearly laughed out loud at the twinkle in her eyes. Their eldest sister did not show charity to anyone. Velma knew Enid lent the coat to keep up appearances. Enid's standards would class lending the fur coat as a major event.

"Thank you, Enid." She leaned across and kissed the older woman's cheek. "I really appreciate your thoughtfulness. Josie has been telling me it can get cold in Aldershot."

"Mind you take good care of it." With a lift of her head Enid left. Once they were sure she had really gone, Velma and Josie fell into each others arms with gales of laughter.

"Is this a private joke or can anyone join in?" Jack asked from the doorway.

Velma quickly explained what had caused the laughter. "Is it time to go?"

"Yes, we need to get there reasonably early. There's a lot of servicemen going to join regiments, or returning from leave. I want to make sure you have a seat. It wouldn't do for you to get too tired."

Josie pulled Velma into her arms. "You have a lovely wedding and come back safe."

"I'll take care of her, Josie. I'll make sure she gets safely on the train back to Plymouth."

Jack picked up Velma's suitcase and took it into the hallway. At the front door Velma gave Josie one last hug, then put her hand in Jack's and walked down the path. As they passed through the gate she turned for one last look. The vision of Josie standing, forlorn, in the doorway trying to keep a brave smile on her face remained with her most of the way to Aldershot.

# Chapter Nine

Jack tried to shield Velma from the crowds on the packed platform. He also needed to hold tight to her so they didn't get separated. The train chugged into the station and when it stopped Jack dragged her with him as he forced his way through to a third class carriage.

"There." He pushed her into a window seat, then put her case in the overhead rack. "Don't you dare move from there or someone will grab the seat."

"What about you?" Velma looked round at the now full seats in the rest of the compartment.

"I'll be all right. If necessary I can always sit in your seat with you on my lap. For the time being I'll sit on the floor."

The whistle blew and the train slowly moved north out of the station. A short while later Jack saw the excitement wear off for Velma. He didn't blame her. The lights in the carriage were dim and the blackout blinds were drawn across the windows. He knew she wouldn't have been able to see anything even if the windows were uncovered. Blackout regulations had been put in place a few days before war had been declared so the whole countryside became invisible at night.

The train stopped at Exeter, then departed on the long trip to Aldershot. The time passed slowly. They were forced to stop at the larger stations and in sidings while they waited for troop trains rushing servicemen from one area to another. Luckily, the boredom made Velma sleepy and she soon nodded off. He rolled up his greatcoat and tucked it under her head to make her more comfortable.

Jack's thoughts turned to the war. Rumours at the camp said it wouldn't last long. Jack didn't know if he believed this. The same things had been said about the 1914 war and the fighting had dragged on for four years. Apprehension mixed with excitement in his stomach as he contemplated the months ahead. As part of the transport division of the RASC, Jack wouldn't be on the front line. He would be pretty close with the support personnel. He'd always wanted to travel. Until he joined up he'd never been far from Hayling Island. Now he would be going overseas. Fighting in a war had not been in his travel plans. Despite this he couldn't help feeling excited about leaving the British Isles.

He stretched to work out the kinks he'd earned from sitting on the floor. The other occupants of the carriage were asleep. This meant Jack could watch Velma as she slept. She looked so beautiful with her natural dark, wavy hair and her fair skin. The warmth of sleep brought a flush to her cheeks. He longed to reach out and stroke her face but didn't want to wake her.

Many hours later, the guard came along the corridor and quietly opened the compartment door.

"Everything all right in here?"

"Yes, thanks. Could you tell me how long it will be until we reach Aldershot?" Jack had no idea where they were. He'd lost track of time with all the stops and starts the train had gone through.

"Should be about forty-five minutes. We've one more stop to make, then the next one will be Aldershot."

"Thank you."

The guard continued on his way. Despite the fact they'd spoken quietly, some of the other travellers stirred. Velma's eyes fluttered open. She stretched and ran the tip of her tongue over her lips.

"I'm sorry. Have I been asleep long?"

"A few hours," Jack patted her knee. "Don't worry about it. You can't see the passing countryside."

Velma caught hold of his hand. They spent rest of the journey in comfortable silence with their hands entwined.

*****

"Aldershot. Aldershot. All change for..."

A string of unintelligible station names followed. Velma didn't pay attention. She concentrated on keeping up with Jack as he pushed his way through the crowd headed for the carriage door. She lost sight of him until she reached the door. He stood on the platform waiting for her. Velma smiled and stepped forward. Someone behind pushed her in the back and she stumbled.

"It's all right, I've got you." Jack's strong arms caught her and he set her down beside him. He carried her suitcase in one hand with Velma catching hold of his other one. He smiled down at her and she knew everything would be all right.

"Jack. Over here."

A blond man in uniform headed for them, his hand raised to catch their attention. This must be the friend from camp Jack had told her about.

"Pete! What are you doing here?"

"There's been a change of plans." Pete led the way out of the station then pulled them to one side, out of the way of the people hurrying in and out of the entrance. To Velma's surprise the clock on the building opposite showed the time as nine o'clock. "We're shipping out tomorrow morning, early."

Velma's heart dropped. They wouldn't be able to be married before Jack went overseas. The journey had been for nothing. She vaguely heard Jack questioning his friend as disappointment washed over her. She needed all her efforts to focus on not breaking down in tears. She must be strong for

Jack.

"That's it then." Jack squeezed her hand. "I'm sorry, Velma. I thought we were all right. It seems we've run out of time."

"Hang on," Pete interrupted. "I've got it all sorted. The registry office can marry you this morning. They were very understanding when I explained the change in plans."

"I suppose half is better than none."

"What do you mean?" Velma frowned.

"We can get married, then I'll have to put you on a train back to Plymouth."

"Will you shut up, Jack." Pete punched his friend in the arm. "I told you it's all arranged."

"And I thank you. At least I can leave knowing Velma is my wife. If we're off early tomorrow, I expect we need to be in barracks early tonight. I have to make sure Velma's safely on her way home first."

"Yes, on the early morning train. Actually, it's at three o'clock in the morning, so it's more like the middle of the night," Pete spoke quickly. "I've been trying to tell you. We have to be in barracks by seven o'clock tonight. I'll go and sign in as myself, next I'll slide under the fence and go back in pretending to be you. When you come back from the station you can climb the fence to get in. They'll never know the difference. They only check to see every name has a signature next to it, and who in their right minds would be climbing into the camp?"

Velma and Jack looked at Pete in amazement. Gradually, Jack's face broke into a smile and he thumped Pete on the back.

"I don't know how to thank you, but I'll find a way."

"One more thing. I changed your booking at the hotel for tonight only. I know you won't be there all night. At least you can have some time alone."

"Thank you." Velma shyly leaned across and kissed Pete's cheek.

"Will you come and be our witness?" Jack asked his friend.

"I'd love to but I have a few things to do before I go back to barracks. Oh, you'll have to wander around a bit until lunchtime. The hotel won't let you have the room until noon. You lovebirds had better get a move on or you'll be late for your own wedding."

Velma could still hear Pete laughing at his own joke as they hurried down the road leading away from the station. The registry office only stood a few roads away from the station. She glanced at the clock in the hall as they entered. They still had half an hour to go before their ten o'clock booking. Jack decided they should sit in the waiting room. It would save them having to drag Velma's suitcase through the streets. Only one other couple were there and Velma wondered if she and Jack appeared as alone and forlorn.

"What are we going to do for witnesses?" she whispered to Jack, afraid of disturbing the forbidding silence.

"Excuse me." Velma jumped as Jack addressed the other couple. He spoke in his normal voice but it sounded loud compared to the previous silence. "Would you mind standing up as our witnesses? We didn't have time to get our family and friends to come."

"Certainly," the man replied. "If you'd be kind enough to do the same for us. We're in the same situation. I'm Dave Hartley and this is my fiancée Sheila Jones."

Velma smiled at Sheila as Jack introduced them. The two men talked of the war. She knew she couldn't find enough courage to begin a conversation with the woman. Sheila evidently had the same problem as she made no move to engage Velma. The pair of them sat in silence waiting their turn in the inner sanctum of the registry office.

The registrar's door burst open and a coupled flushed with happiness erupted followed by beaming friends and family. Velma watched wistfully as the wedding party noisily disappeared through the big outer doors. It would have been so nice to have Florence and Josie there. She shook these thoughts from her mind as Dave and Sheila were called forward. She and Jack followed to witness the marriage.

"Mr. Hartley and Miss Jones, if I might see your documentation." The Registrar checked their paperwork then entered their details in the register.

The Registrar indicated where they should stand and asked the couple to declare they knew of no reason why they should not be lawfully married to each other. Once the other couple had done this they said their vows agreeing to take each other as husband and wife.

"Do you have any additional vows you'd like to make? No, then you may exchange rings." The Registrar paused while Dave placed a ring on Sheila's hand. His bride didn't have a ring for her groom so the ceremony continued. "I now pronounce you husband and wife. If you would please sign the register."

Velma watched with interest as the couple went through their ceremony and she happily stepped forward to sign as a witness. Now, she and Jack handed over their documents. Thankfully all the necessary paperwork and rings had been organised for their white wedding. They'd only needed to obtain a special licence. Documents checked, they stood where the Registrar told them.

"Do you Velma Field know of any reason why you should not take Jack Stanley as your lawful wedded husband?"

"No."

The Registrar repeated the question to Jack with the names reversed. He also answered in the negative.

"Have either of you any additional vows you would like to make?"

"It's not a vow. I would like to say something to my bride."

Velma blinked with surprise. Jack hadn't mentioned saying anything additional. The Registrar nodded to indicate Jack should go ahead.

"Velma, I know this isn't the wedding we planned. I want you to know my vows to you are the most important part of us getting married. I love you and although I have to leave you soon to go and do my part for our country, you will always be in my thoughts. I hope this war will be over soon so we can start our married life together."

Tears blurred Velma's vision. She threw her arms around Jack and kissed him.

"Ahem, perhaps the exchange of rings should come first," the Registrar suggested.

A short time later the new Mr. and Mrs. Hartley and even newer Mr. and Mrs. Stanley left the imposing building. A bitter wind blew as they reached the pavement outside. Velma hugged Enid's fur coat more closely round her shoulders to keep herself warm.

"Do you want to get a bite at a café?" Dave Hartley asked. "We all have to eat and it could be an impromptu wedding breakfast."

"Sounds good," Jack replied. Velma almost voiced a protest. They only had a short time together -- how could Jack waste their precious time? Then she remembered the hotel wouldn't let them have their room until twelve. "We've got an hour or two to spare before we can get into our room."

Velma had planned to enjoy a more posh menu than fish and chips and a pot of tea on her wedding day. Despite this, she quite enjoyed the meal and it filled up the hungry space inside her. No food had passed her lips since the meal Josie made her eat last night. Once again the men talked about the war. Velma made an effort to communicate with Sheila. Although they were strangers, they had witnessed each others wedding.

"I come from Plymouth. Did you have to travel far to get to Aldershot?"

"Not really. My home's in Southampton."

Velma wondered if she lived so close why her family hadn't attended the wedding. She pushed the thought from her mind.

"Lucky you. I've got a full night's travel before I get home. I didn't find it too bad coming up here. Jack took good care of me. Hopefully there won't be so many people going the other way."

"I'm staying in Aldershot. I haven't got any family. Dave is based here for the time being so I'm going to live in digs until we know where he's going to be sent."

*Well that answers that question.* Relief washed over Velma. *Thank goodness I didn't ask why she had been alone with Dave.*

The clock struck noon as they finished their meal. They all stood up and the two men shook hands while the women smiled at one another.

"Maybe see you around the camp sometime."

"I think we're shipping out soon," Jack replied.

Velma kept the frown from her face. *Why didn't Jack say he's leaving tonight?*

"Jack..." she glanced up at him as they walked along the street.

"I know what you're going to say, my love. I'll explain when we get to the hotel."

They didn't have far to go until they entered the hotel foyer through the swing doors. Delicious warmth enfolded them. Velma glanced around her, amazed at the opulent surroundings. She'd only ever stayed in houses belonging to relatives when she'd been away from home. The reception area would have been more suited to a scene from a film. The curved staircase and plush furnishings all looked expensive. The crystal chandelier hanging from the ceiling would probably have cost the same as Josie and Will's house.

Jack led her up to the reception desk, placing her suitcase on the floor beside him. They waited politely for the lady behind the desk to notice them. She peered at them over the top of her glasses. Velma got the impression she thought they weren't good enough for the hotel.

"Mr. and Mrs. Stanley. We have a room booked for one night."

The woman sniffed and ran her finger down the list on the page in front of her.

"Room sixteen. Payment in advance please."

Velma would have liked to give the woman a piece of her mind. They were paying for the room with cash and should receive the same level of respect as other, better off guests. She didn't want to spoil her wedding day, so she kept quiet as Jack paid and the woman reluctantly handed over the key.

"Thank you. Have a pleasant day." Jack picked up the case and smiled at Velma as they walked away.

She glanced over her shoulder. The woman at least had the decency to blush for her rude behaviour.

*****

Jack put the key in the lock of room sixteen and opened the door with a flourish. He stopped Velma before she could enter.

"We have to keep up with tradition." He scooped her into his arms and carried her across the threshold. As he lowered her to the floor, his arms pulled her close. "Hello Mrs. Stanley. Have I told you today how much I love you?"

"I'm not sure, tell me again." He hugged her as she laughed softly. "I know I love you so much, my darling Jack."

"I love you, too."

The kiss he placed on her lips went on for a long time. Only a discreet cough at the door pulled them apart. He'd been so keen on doing things right he'd forgotten to close the door behind them. He'd also left Velma's suitcase in the hallway. An elderly housemaid stood outside with a fond smile on her face.

"I have a bowl of fruit for Mr. and Mrs. Stanley. A young man brought them by earlier."

"Probably from Pete," Jack told Velma. He crossed the room and gave the woman sixpence as he took the bowl from her. "Thank you very much for delivering this."

He scooped up the suitcase and shut the door behind him.

"Jack, why did you tell David you thought you'd be shipping out soon?"

"We've been told not to say too much about when and where we're going. You never know who the enemy is. Same as I won't be able to tell you where I am when I write to you. You'll know though by some of the comments I make."

"Such as?" Velma's puzzled expression showed the thoughts going through her mind. How could he tell her his location if the censor would remove any mention of where he was?

"What if I wrote and told you I'd seen Aunty Lily's son, what would you think?"

"I'd think you'd gone mad. To my knowledge neither of us have an Aunty Lily."

"Precisely. So think of a place sounding like Lily. Lille is a place in France, so you'd know where I'd been."

"Oh, I see. How clever. I must make sure I've got an atlas so I can look up the words that don't make sense."

Jack smiled at her and moved towards her. He noticed Velma shifted away uncertainty.

"What's the matter? You're not having regrets about a big wedding are you?"

"No of course not. It's just -- well I--"

"Please, Velma. You're worrying me. What's bothering you?"

"The wedding night."

The words came from her in a burst and at first Jack didn't understand what she meant. Then it dawned on him. He had a virgin bride. She came from a large family, so surely she knew what went on between husband and wife.

"Don't worry, my darling. There's no need to be frightened. I'll be gentle with you. It might hurt a bit at first, but that part will be over quickly." He reached for her. She backed away from him again.

"I'm not worried about making love, Jack. I trust you. Won't people know what we're doing if we stay in our room all afternoon? It will be so embarrassing and in any case it's not decent."

Laughter rumbled in his chest. He sobered at the deadly serious expression on her face.

"Velma, let them think whatever they want to. You'll probably never see them again. What's more important is for you and me to become truly married in every sense of the word before I go away. Whoever told you it isn't decent for a man to make love to his wife in the afternoon -- well they must be daft."

"Let's go for a walk first and have a cup of tea. We probably won't have time later so maybe we could get some sandwiches to eat for supper."

"Good idea." Jack knew Velma would feel more settled if he took things at her pace. She had also made a good suggestion. They would need to keep out of sight from sunset until the time arrived for him to take her to the station. He didn't know for sure, but he had a feeling the redcaps might be out collecting stragglers in the early evening. Hopefully, by the time they left to put Velma on the train, there wouldn't be too many around.

Jack took her hand in his and they walked down the stairs to the lobby. The receptionist glanced towards them and quickly returned to the paperwork on her desk. He hid a smile. No doubt the woman tried to hide her embarrassment at the way she'd treated them when they'd signed in.

Fingers linked they wandered around the town and Jack pointed out a few places of interest. They stopped at a small café for afternoon tea and ordered sandwiches to take away. By the time they returned to the hotel the sun had begun to set. When at last the door of their room shut behind them, Jack turned to face Velma.

"Would you like me to leave the room for a while?" Hesitation shook his normally calm voice. "I mean if you want to get changed."

He longed to take Velma in his arms and tenderly make love to her. Did she feel the same? She might want to change into her night gear first.

"I would like to get changed." Velma smiled at him. Jack nodded and turned to leave the room. "No wait, Jack. There's no need for you to go. There's a screen in the corner, I can hop behind there to get ready."

With a kiss on his cheek, Velma took some things from her case and went behind the screen. Jack didn't know what he should do. He would look an idiot if he still had all his clothes on when she returned. He quickly removed his shirt, shoes and socks then debated whether to take off his trousers and vest. No -- it wouldn't take too long to divest himself of these at the appropriate moment. If he stripped completely he would embarrass Velma.

To calm his mind from the anticipation of what he hoped would happen Jack looked out the window at the evening sky. The stars were just beginning to emerge from the darkening canopy. A flash of silver shot across the sky. Jack usually didn't pay attention to superstitious beliefs but the shooting star indicated a good beginning to his marriage. He fervently prayed he and Velma would have a long and happy life ahead of them despite the war.

*****

Behind the screen Velma found a basin and ewer of water. She quickly removed her clothes and sponged herself all over then dried with the towel provided. She dabbed a drop of lavender water behind the ears, under her breasts and inside her wrists. Then she slipped into her night clothes.

Josie sewed the nightdress and negligee for her as a wedding present. Velma had never seen anything so pretty. White lawn cotton so thin it floated; delicate Honiton lace edged the neck and sleeves with a deeper layer along the bottom of the nightdress.

Part of Velma wanted to hurry out to Jack, while her nerves urged her to stay behind the screen. She took a deep breath and forced her feet to move. She entered the main part of the room to find Jack with his back to her. Through the window she could see the sky had darkened and the stars were now visible.

"Jack, I'm ready." Her soft words broke the silence. Jack pulled down the blackout and closed the curtains before turning away from the window.

His breath caught in his throat as he looked at her. His gaze raked her from head to toe, taking in every detail of her body.

"My Velma. My beautiful Velma."

She didn't see him move. Suddenly his arms were around her and his lips were on hers. Her body melted into his embrace and feelings she'd only dreamed of rushed through her being, switching off any thought of resistance. Nervous laughter bubbled up inside. Resist -- she intended to make passionate love with her new husband, resistance had no place in her mind.

Jack picked her up in his arms. He swept the covers back and placed her on the bed. Her eyes followed him as he moved around to the other side. She frowned when he paused before joining her. He reached for his trousers. Velma quickly turned away as he removed his remaining clothes.

The mattress dipped as Jack climbed into the bed. He pulled her to him. Velma gazed at his face. A deep glow of love shone in his eyes as he traced his finger down the contours of her face.

Breathless, Velma gave herself up to his kiss. He caressed her neck and moved towards her breasts.

"Your skin is so soft and silky," he whispered as he gently stroked her. He raised his head and looked down at her. "Do you mind if I take this off?"

He lifted a fold of her nightdress. Velma had never been naked in front of another woman, let alone a man. She nodded nervously and held her breath. Jack drew the hem of the garment over her head. Her eyes slammed shut as she heard his indrawn breath. Deep inside she wanted Jack to make passionate love to her, but her emotions found it difficult to cope with the reality. She held herself rigid knowing his gaze roamed over her body. He touched her. Velma's nerves were so tight she nearly screamed with fright.

*Maybe I should open my eyes. No, I'd be so embarrassed to see him looking at me in all my glory.*

He stroked her skin with tender fingertips, moving from her shoulders to her breast. Once again a thrill of excitement rushed through her as he brushed against her nipple. His lips touched hers, gently at first then with more and more passion. Velma responded with equal fervour. His hands were now stroking her stomach and her body reacted instantly. Ripples of warmth ran up and down her nerves to join the tingle between her thighs, encouraging the warm moisture building up there.

Jack's head dipped to her breasts and his tongue licked her nipple, then he nibbled the same spot. Her body arched towards him, encouraging Jack to move to the other nipple. Desire shot through Velma, followed by more waves of warmth and excitement.

*Oh my God, I'm losing my mind.* Jack moved down to her stomach dropping little kisses as he went. *My body's not my own any more. Stop. No don't stop. Oh God.*

Velma lost all sense of herself. Caught up in the passion, when Jack moved on top of her, she threw her arms around him and pulled him closer. For a moment, intense pain shot through her and she gasped. Jack continued and the pain disappeared in the waves of pleasure overtaking her body, sending her into a spiral of emotions exploding into a rainbow in her mind.

\*\*\*\*\*

Jack found it hard to restrain himself. To look at Velma excited him. To see her naked, lying on the bed waiting for him, had strained his need to control himself. His own excitement grew as Velma's body reacted to his stroking and kissing.

He entered her and she gasped with pain. For a moment he considered stopping, but his body overruled him. He tried hard to be gentle. He surprised himself. He didn't find this difficult. Before he'd met Velma, he'd participated in the visits to town with the other lads to visit the very willing ladies of the night. Tonight had been completely different.

He and Velma climaxed at the same time and he flopped down beside her on the mattress. He glanced over at his bride. She lay with her eyes closed and a dreamy expression on her face. Jack smiled, pleased her first experience with lovemaking had ended so well.

The difference! It had to be lovemaking. Before he'd had sex. The reason for the different feeling came from love. He loved Velma and had made love to her, emotionally as well as physically. He turned on his side, his arm leaning on the pillow supporting his head. The other hand stroked her arm following the outline of the soft skin. Velma shifted and turned towards him. His breath caught in his throat at the willingness in her eyes. He reached for her and she moved into his arms and his embrace.

# Chapter Ten

Lost in thought, Velma sat in the third class carriage on the Exeter to Plymouth train. Her mind focused on the wonderful, short, time she and Jack had spent together. She didn't know when she'd see him again, but hoped it wouldn't be too long. The train steamed slowly into Plymouth Station and she gathered her case from the overhead rack. Florence and Sam stood on the platform. The boy caught sight of her and he waved enthusiastically. Velma smiled. She'd been met by members of both her family and Jack's.

A shiver passed over her as she stepped down on the platform. Nothing would really change. She'd go back to work and carry on living with Josie and Tom. The only difference would be her surname. This is how she and Jack had planned it. They'd decided not to get a place of their own. It would be a waste of money as Jack didn't think he would be back for some time. Velma would stay in her room at Josie's until he returned. All the same Velma couldn't help feeling disappointed. She'd feel she and Jack had never been married if nothing changed.

"Aunty Vee," Sam flung his arms around her. "Mummy says you're twice my aunty now."

The boy stood back and looked at her critically, a frown furrowing his brow. Velma smiled, guessing what he would say next.

"You don't look any bigger, Aunty Vee."

"I'm not bigger, sweetheart. Mummy means I can love you twice as much now."

Sam thought about this for a moment, then a brilliant smile broke across his face. He threw his arms around Velma again.

"And I love you twice as much, Aunty Vee."

The two women smiled and hugged, and each held one of Sam's hands. They headed for the exit with the boy bouncing up and down between them.

"Everything go all right?" Florence asked.

"It went really well," Velma answered. "We'd rather have had the family there but it wasn't to be. We had to bring the wedding forward a day as well. Wait a minute. How did you know I'd be on this train? I told Josie I wouldn't be coming back until tomorrow."

"Jack sent George a telegram from the hotel telling us what train you'd be on."

A shadow crossed Florence's face as she spoke of George.

"What's wrong, Florence? Nothing's happened to George has it?" She spoke in a low voice, not wanting to upset Sam.

"George has got his orders. He's to report to the barracks at Exeter next Sunday, so he'll leave early Sunday morning." Florence spoke equally quiet.

"Oh, Florence."

"Shh!" Florence nodded her head towards her son. "We're going to have a lovely few days before he goes. I don't know when we'll see him again. George thinks he'll be sent overseas."

They walked in silence. Velma wondered how many others would leave their wives and children behind while they went off to fight in the war. She shuddered as her thoughts continued -- how many of those men would not return at the end of the fighting?

"Velma, I want to ask you something. I don't want you to reply right away. I'd like you to think about what I say before you give me an answer."

"Don't sound so serious, Florence. It can't be that bad."

"It's not. At least I hope you won't think it's bad. George and I talked it over and he's not happy with me being in the house on my own with Sam. We wondered if you would like to move in with us. It would be company for me and Sam would love to have his Aunty Vee at his beck and call. You could have the box room."

Velma looked at her sister in astonishment. She had been given the perfect excuse to move out of Josie's without upsetting the sister who'd been like a mother to her. Not that she didn't like it there. If she lived with Florence it would make her feel life really had changed when she got married. Besides, she could help with Sam. Such a dear little boy, but like all children he could be a handful at times, especially now as he grew older.

"Florence, I don't have to think about it. I'd love to come and live with you. Jack and I can't afford to get a place of our own. If I go back to Josie and Tom I would feel I haven't got married." Velma giggled. "People will get very confused with two Mrs. Stanleys at the same address. What do you think Josie will say?"

"I've already spoken to Josie so she knows we haven't gone behind her back. She understood why I wanted to ask you. She said the final decision must be up to you." Florence grinned. "She actually said you're not a child anymore and quite capable of making up your own mind."

"Good, that's the reason I'll use."

Sam had been quiet while they discussed the living arrangements. Now he showed his boredom. Twisting his hands free he ran off down the road and both women chased him. He turned in through a garden gate and Velma stopped running and laughed. They were home.

"I didn't realise we were quite so close. Sam obviously did. I guess you'll have to come in for a cup of tea now."

Arm in arm they walked round to the back of the house. They entered by the kitchen door and smiled at Josie. She'd placed a biscuit and a glass of milk in front of Sam who sat at the kitchen table.

"I knew you two wouldn't be far behind when this young scamp charged through the door nearly knocking me over." She looked keenly at Velma. "How did the wedding go? Why are you home a day early?"

"Jack's embarkation has been brought forward so we had to move the wedding up as well," Velma told her. "We got married yesterday and Jack put me on the early morning train then went back to barracks. I'm not sure where he is by now."

"Take your case up to your room and then come down for a cup of tea." Josie shooed her towards the doorway.

Velma climbed the stairs and put her case on the bed. Before returning downstairs she stood in the middle of the room and looked around. This had been the only place she'd ever been able to be alone. The only room in the house she could truly call hers. With a shake of her head she went back to the kitchen to face Josie and explain why she wanted to go and live with Florence.

"So you see, Josie, I'd not only be helping Florence, but it would also give me a chance to grow up. I've always lived here and I'm the youngest sister so the others still treat me like a child. If I go to live with Florence, they'll have to stop interfering in my life and you won't have to worry I'm living alone or with strangers."

Velma held her breath. Would Josie understand her, or would she think Velma had made up an excuse.

"I do believe you're right." Josie had a thoughtful look in her eyes. "You're my little sister. I've tried to treat you like a young working woman. Enid, on the other hand, still thinks she can tell you, and the rest of us, what to do. You'll be striking a bid for freedom for all of us if you move in with Florence."

"You needn't think you're getting rid of me either. I'll come round and see you often." Velma flung her arms around Josie and hugged the older woman.

"So when would you like to move in?" Florence asked.

Velma considered the question for a moment. "Would Sunday suit you? I'll be back at work tomorrow and I'll need time to sort through my things and pack them. I have to change my name on all the official stuff, plus Jack's given me a form to lodge with the RASC to show I'm his wife. I can change my address the same time I alter my surname. If we say Sunday, you won't have to spend a night on your own. Tom can give me a hand with the heavier stuff." A thought hit her like a lightning bolt and she spun round to Josie. "He hasn't been called up has he?"

"No. Tom's job is a reserved occupation, and he's also just over the age limit to serve. Not that he wouldn't go like a shot if they asked him."

"Don't tell him I said so, but I'm glad he's not going. We need at least one man around the place. I suppose John's rushed off to fight." Velma knew her brother. His patriotic duty would lead him to defend his country in whatever capacity he could, especially as their father had died in the Great War.

"He's signed up, but doesn't leave until next week so you'll have time to say goodbye."

Florence and Sam went home. Velma helped Josie clear the table and prepare lunch. Later she went in to work to advise them she'd be returning the following day, then on to the various government departments to change her details and register herself as Mrs. Jack Stanley. Each time she wrote her new name she shivered with the thrill of being Jack's wife.

*****

"What's it like being a married woman?" Gladdie linked arms with her as they made their way up the staff stairs.

"No different than being single. Jack's still away--" Velma grinned.

"And you're still living at home. Never mind, they say the war will soon be over, then you and Jack can start married life for real."

"I wouldn't believe all you hear about the war being over soon. They said the same thing the last time and it went on for four years." Velma's stomach churned. Last time she'd lost her father. This time she hoped it wouldn't be her husband who died. She pushed the disturbing thought to the back of her mind. "Anyway, I won't be living at Josie's for much longer."

"What do you mean? You're not moving to Aldershot are you?"

"Aldershot? Why would I move there? Oh, you mean move due to Jack being stationed there." Velma laughed. "I don't know if he'll come back there. I meant I'm moving in with Florence on Sunday. George is going off to fight and she doesn't want to be on her own."

"What do the sisters say about that?"

Velma carefully considered Gladdie's question. What would the sisters say? Did it matter what they said? No, she decided. She no longer had to answer to them about her life and what she intended to do.

"They don't know yet. It doesn't make any difference though. They can't order me around anymore. They've been ruling my life for too long. I worried about upsetting Josie, but she thinks it's a good idea."

"Do you need a hand moving?"

"No, thanks. Florence is going to bring round Sam's old pram on Sunday. We should be able to get everything in. I haven't really got that much. If necessary we'll make two trips."

The bell rang reminding staff to take their positions behind the counter. Both women hurried down the stairs to begin the working day.

Sunday came all too quickly. They had decided to get the moving done in the morning to present a *fait accompli* to the sisters when they came for afternoon tea. Florence arrived on the stroke of nine o'clock and they loaded up the pram.

"Now you leave Sam here with me," Josie ordered. "I need his help to make some cakes. Would you like to help me, Sam?"

The little boy jumped up and down at the offer to help with the baking. Too excited to talk, he nodded wordlessly.

"You be a good boy for Aunty Josie." His mother kissed his cheek. "Aunty Vee and I won't be long."

Sam had no time for his mother's kisses. He eagerly carried ingredients to the table to make the cakes. Velma and Florence laughed as they pushed the pram down the street. They took the short cut through Victoria Park and were soon unloading Velma's belongings into her new bedroom.

"I'll tidy it up later," she told Florence as they surveyed the pile of books and personal belongings. The clothes had been hung up straight away to make sure they didn't crease.

The two sisters talked about the afternoon meeting with the family as they walked back to Josie's.

"I bet Enid has something to say. She always has to have the last word."

"I must remember to give her back her fur coat," Velma said. "Do you know this is the first time I've known her do something nice without being asked."

"She hasn't always been like she is now. I think when our father died and then mum couldn't cope, poor Enid had to become the matriarch of the family. John couldn't take charge at his age. Enid had her own husband and children and the war had only just finished. She made sure everyone got taken care of. I guess she's fallen into the habit of telling us all what to do."

"The trouble is we let her get away with it and when we stand up to her, she doesn't like it." Velma agreed with her sister. "She's going to get another shock this afternoon isn't she? This must be the third time I've stood up to her in the last year."

Arm in arm the sisters walked through the park and made their way to Josie's home in Wyndham Street. They were met by Sam, covered in flour, but with a supremely happy smile on his face.

"I made cakes," he announced proudly. "Lots of cakes."

"Good boy," his mother hugged him. "Are they for afternoon tea?"

"Yes, Mummy. Aunty Josie let me eat one. She said we had to make sure they tasted right."

"And did the cake taste right?"

"Great." Sam licked his lips and his mother laughed.

Velma joined in the laughter then excused herself. "I just want to make sure I haven't forgotten anything,"

She sat on the bed in her old room, now stripped of its bedding. She looked around the room, so bare without her personal belongings. Her whole life had been spent within these four walls. The wardrobe, washstand and bed had been there as long as she could remember. The short move to Florence's really made her feel a married woman.

"Velma, lunch is ready."

Josie's call brought Velma out of her reverie and she left the room without glancing back.

*****

"Ready?" Velma watched Josie twist the tea towel in her hands.

"I guess so." Josie swallowed. "They'll be here soon, won't they?"

"Don't worry, Josie. They can't say I'm their responsibility now I'm married." Velma gave her sister a big hug as the front door banged. "Go put the kettle on, I'll confront the family."

To her relief Florence came through the doorway. She and Sam had popped back home to fetch Florence's contribution to the afternoon tea.

"Where's Josie?"

"She's gone to put the kettle on." Both sisters glanced toward the hall as the front door opened again.

"I think I'll join her." Florence quickly disappeared into the kitchen.

Enid entered the room first, with two other sisters trailing behind her.

"John's gone to join the other men." Enid settled herself in the most comfortable chair. Velma had to hide a smile as the others settled beside her like broody hens.

"There are no men but John," she informed Enid. "George has gone off to camp and Tom is helping sort out the wardens."

Enid sniffed in a disapproving manner. The men of the family had no right being out when they knew she'd be visiting. Velma had a sinking feeling in her stomach as Enid turned in her direction.

"Well, it's nice to see you came back safely. How did the wedding go?"

"Very well, thank you. Oh, that reminds me." Velma indicated the fur coat hanging on a hanger from the hook behind the door. "Thank you so much for lending me your coat. It kept me lovely and warm. Exactly what I needed and I made sure to take good care when I wore it."

"Couldn't have you getting married looking like a pauper." Enid sniffed. Her gaze flicked to the coat and Velma once again hid a smile. She knew as soon as her sister got home the coat would suffer intense scrutiny to make sure nothing had happened to it.

"We got married earlier than planned. Jack's company had orders to be confined to barracks so we brought the wedding forward a day."

"You mean you've been home for two days and you didn't think to contact any of us?"

"I went back to work, Enid. Then I had to fill in forms about changing my name."

"Changing your name to what, may I ask?"

"To Stanley. When I married Jack I became Velma Stanley."

"You should still have found time to let us know you were back." Enid's face held an expression her sisters all dreaded. Velma called it the 'I know best' look.

"I also had to change my address details." Velma held her breath, waiting for the explosion.

"Why? Isn't this house good enough for you? I suppose you're getting ideas above your station now you're a married woman. Are you sure Jack would approve of you setting up on your own?"

Velma decided she'd had enough of Enid's dictatorial ways. She took a deep breath to keep her voice sounding calm.

"First, it is no concern of yours where I live. Second, while I am touched by your concern for me, I am now a married woman and quite capable of making up my own mind. In fact, this has been the case for some time. Lastly, my new address will be care of Mrs. George Stanley."

"Florence? Why are you going to live with Florence?"

Unnoticed by Velma, Florence and Josie had entered the room behind her. She turned as Florence spoke.

"Velma moved in as a favour to me. George left this morning. He didn't like leaving Sam and me on our own. Velma kindly agreed to keep me company."

"I think it's a lovely idea. They'll be good for one another." Josie looked shocked that she'd spoken out against Enid.

"You mean you've already moved?" Enid appeared to be extremely put out.

"I had no reason to wait and I have to work tomorrow." Velma kept her face straight as she spoke to her oldest sister. "Now, let's have tea shall we?"

Josie whispered Tom had returned so the men were out in the back yard enjoying a smoke. The two sisters who had arrived with Enid gave Velma a nod of respect as they passed her. Nobody had dared to stand up to Enid before.

*****

Velma sat in her new room that night writing to Jack before she went to bed. She described Enid's chagrin at not being able to have things her own way.

"...in some ways it's a little sad, Jack. She didn't know what to say and nobody backed her up like usual. Do you know, I think she's secretly relieved? Ever since my father died she's ruled the family. I suppose she thought she had to. Now I'm married she can let go. I shall try to be nicer to her next time I see her..."

The letter continued with a reminder for him to write to her at Florence's address, and ended with Velma sending her love to her darling husband. She sealed the envelope and got ready for bed. Velma guessed she'd get used to undressing in an unfamiliar room.

She snuggled down in the strange bed and her thoughts turned to the afternoon. The move to Florence's had gone without a hitch and Enid reluctantly accepted the inevitable. From now on Velma intended to be treated as an adult and Jack's wife, not the little sister who needed to be protected.

Blackouts covered the windows of her new bedroom, keeping it dark. She wondered about Jack's whereabouts at this moment. By now he should be in Europe, but she didn't know where. Until his company got to its destination, he wouldn't be able to give her any hints. Thoughts of Jack lifted her spirits, making her ecstatically happy. He might be on the other side of the English Channel by now. Her excitement disappeared. Over there he would come face to face with the enemy and be expected to fight, maybe kill. Or the enemy soldiers could kill Jack.

Velma longed for a letter from him, but, of course, he didn't know she'd moved in with Florence. Josie had promised to bring round any letters as soon as they arrived. Hopefully, her own mail wouldn't take too long to get to him.

# Chapter Eleven

*October 1939*

Jack sat with the blank piece of paper in front of him. Instead of the cheap notepaper he envisaged Velma's face as she had looked when she slept beside him the night of their wedding day. He longed to hold her in his arms again, but knew it would be many months before that would be possible.

Enough of this daydreaming, he had to get his letter written to catch the outgoing mail.

*My darling Velma,*

*I miss you so much my love. It helps to know you're safe at home. I received your letters and will send this to Florence's address. It's nice the two of you are together. You'll be able to support one another and keep your spirits up. I'd love to have seen the expression on Enid's face when you stood up to her. Well done, my darling.*

*We've been travelling through some beautiful countryside, it's hard to realise we're at war. Then you see the troops moving all over the place complete with all the things needed to fight the enemy and you realise it's only the calm before the storm.*

*I met up with Aunt Lily's boy the other day. Didn't know he'd joined up.*

Jack grinned. He'd used the same example to explain to Velma how she'd know where he would be and then they'd actually gone through the town.

*The weather hasn't been that brilliant but I'm managing. We've had a few troubles with the vehicles. They're sorted now. I wonder if you could send me some thick socks and notepaper so I can keep warm and write to you.*

*Can't tell you much about where I am as it's not a good idea to put anything down on paper. Must away, my love, sorry I haven't much to tell you. Must get this in the envelope quickly as the mail will be going soon. Take care of yourself, my darling, and remember I love you so very much.*

*Jack*
*xxxxxxx*

He quickly sealed the envelope and hurried out into the rain to the mail tent. He dropped the letter into the outgoing sack, knowing the censors would pore over it with their blacking machines before it reached Velma. They diligently did their job, taking out anything that indicated progression of the war.

Hands in pockets he slouched back to his tent, dipping his head to try and stop getting too wet. He passed Pete, who slapped him cheerfully on the back.

"What's the matter, Jack? Missing the new Mrs. Stanley? How is the lovely bride?"

"Velma's fine." Pride welled up inside Jack when he heard Velma referred to as '*Mrs. Stanley*'. "She's moved in with her sister, my brother George's wife. They'll be company for each other."

"And your sister-in-law can keep an eye on her to make sure she doesn't find some sailor to keep her warm," Pete joked.

"Velma's not like that." For a moment Jack's anger flashed. He wouldn't even let his best friend make coarse remarks about his wife. "She'll wait for me, no matter how long this war takes."

"Rumour is we'll be moving out again soon. Wish this dratted rain would stop. It makes the lorries bog down and then it's the devil to get them moving again."

Jack agreed, relieved his friend had changed the subject. He would warn Pete later not to talk about Velma in a bad way. The woman he loved must be spoken of with respect.

Day followed day as they slogged through the rain. The lorries and other vehicles kept sticking in the mud. They spent hours dragging and pushing to free them. Days turned into weeks and all too soon Christmas arrived.

Mail came on Christmas Eve and Jack had a parcel from Velma and another from his mother. He kept them until Christmas Day. When he opened them he smiled. The two women had obviously been in touch with each other. Ma had sent him several pairs of knitted socks and Velma had included the notepaper he'd requested, plus a tin of talcum powder.

Ma had always told her children if they got their feet wet to dry them between the toes and sprinkle with powder. This apparently stopped any problems. He pulled off his boots and stripped the socks from his feet. Using the dirty socks he followed his mother's instructions and dried his feet. Next he sprinkled them with Velma's powder. To his surprise his feet felt much better.

*Darling Velma,*

*Thank you so much for the notepaper and talcum powder. Ma sent some knitted socks so I managed to make my feet comfortable for the first time in I don't know how long. Christmas passed very quietly here. We didn't move and for once it stopped raining. Hopefully, the weather will get better now we're starting a new year.*

*Nancy wrote the other day...*

Would she understand he wrote to her from Nance? Of course she would, his beautiful Velma had brains.

*...nice to hear from her.*

*Hope everyone in the family is well especially George and John. I'm keeping well and think of you a lot. I miss you so much, my Velma. I'm not sure when I'll be home again but it can't be soon enough for me.*

*Take care, my darling. I love you so very, very much.*

*Your besotted husband,*
*Jack*
*xxxxx*

The New Year passed and Jack thought their whole journey a pointless exercise. They moved round in circles. Going one place, moving on to the next and eventually coming back to the first location confused him. He couldn't work out the places they'd already visited and those they hadn't.

"Jack, do you think we're heading back north?"

"What makes you say that, Pete?"

"Think of all the places we've been to recently. We passed through them when we were coming south. Stands to reason if we're going through them in reverse order we must be heading back to the coast."

For a few moments Jack went over their recent route. Pete could be right. They were visiting places they'd been before, but going the other way.

"Do you think we're heading home?"

"Maybe, I'm not sure. Even if we are, at the speed we're moving it will take us forever to get there."

The two of them laughed and returned to their work.

A few days later they turned south again and the two friends shook their heads. The powers that be must know what they were doing. Shame nobody thought to divulge the reasons to the men who were actually carrying out the orders.

At the end of the week they were still moving through the boggy terrain when the convoy had orders to halt. The captain came down the line and told all the drivers they were heading back north to the coast.

"What the blazes is going on, Jack? First one way, then the other? Any ideas?"

"Maybe the enemy's closer than they thought. Or could be they sent us the wrong way in the first place. Doesn't do to figure out why. My mum's got a saying. 'Ours is not to reason why, ours is just to do or die'."

"Very cheerful," Pete said with a grin. "Just what I wanted to hear when we might be surrounded by the enemy."

"Here we go."

Jack swung the steering wheel as the soldier at the side of the road beckoned him to turn round. Within minutes they were going over the same road they'd travelled the day before. The convoy didn't stop that night, it carried on relentlessly. Jack wondered when they would get to rest. It had been a long day and the light had already faded. At last they pulled into a muddy field in the middle of nowhere. The men were too tired to complain, they could barely swallow the food rations handed out and went to sleep in their lorries for the night.

Many times over the following months Jack wondered at the purpose behind their travels. They went one way, then turned back on their tracks. No explanations were given, but the rumour merchants were rife with what could be happening.

Velma wrote often and he responded, trying to put as much of his love into the words as he could. She sent him all the news of Sam, what George had said in his letters to Florence and Tom's frustration. Poor man, they wouldn't let him join up. When the government upped the age limit, he'd got permission to resign from his job only to find he couldn't pass the medical. Apparently, a childhood illness had left him with a weak heart. Poor Tom had been forced to stay in his reserved occupation. He made up for it by becoming a fire warden.

Jack noticed the last few days they were heading nearer to the coast. They had been fired on several times over the months of travelling round Europe. Now the gunfire intensified. The convoy headed for the coast and just before they pulled off the road for the night he noticed a signpost. Dunkirk lay only a few miles away.

*****

"Letters, Aunty Vee."

Sam's excited yell had Velma hurrying down the hall to the kitchen. Three letters lay on the kitchen table. Addressed to her, they all had the "Passed Censor" stamp blazoned across the envelope. She picked them up and looked at Florence.

"Go on," her sister said. "The meal won't be ready for another half an hour. Go and read your letters."

"Thanks, Florence."

Velma ran upstairs to her room. Without even taking her coat off she sat down on the bed and carefully opened the letter with the oldest date stamp.

Jack's handwriting tumbled over the page, telling her how he'd spent his days. Not specifically where, but he'd been driving and mending vehicles and getting stuck in mud. She grinned. She didn't mind how much mud he encountered as long as he didn't get involved in the fighting. Jack never mentioned any heavy artillery or tanks, but she knew he must be near to the battlefields. Someone had to keep the lorries and tanks on the road, and this job belonged to the RASC. She appreciated how he tried to protect her. She worried all the same. The other two letters were only slightly different in content to the first.

Velma enjoyed living with Florence. Sam made the war seem more distant with his constant chatter and joy of life. She found the sisters now treated her as an adult rather than a child who constantly needed to be told what to do.

She pulled the brush through her wavy hair and tripped down the stairs to help Florence with the meal preparations. Her sister had already set the table with the vegetable pie in pride of place in the centre.

"Good job George planted the garden before he left. At least we won't go short of fresh vegetables."

Sam chattered away as they ate and the sisters smiled at each other across the boy's head. The food tasted delicious and Velma appreciated her sister's ability to manage on such short rations.

After the meal they cleared up and put Sam to bed. The two sisters sat down with their knitting to listen to the radio. The news didn't report much. Despite the government's request for people not to start rumours, the public knew the exact details of shortages and troop movements.

"Rationing's getting worse," Florence commented. "I got less meat today and if not for Sam we wouldn't be getting any eggs at all."

"We'll just have to have black tea then."

"If we've got any tea. They're rationing that, too."

Christmas came and went with Sam being the centre of attention in the Stanley household. Velma and her sisters managed to find Christmas presents for the nieces and nephews, although most were homemade. The Sunday afternoon teas were infrequent, they had nothing to share. Everything they could find in the shops they needed in their own homes.

January passed into February and February into March. News from the front didn't sound good. The closeness of the war to the British Isles hit home in the middle of the month.

Velma arrived home breathless, having run all the way from work.

"Florence, did you hear? The Germans have bombed Scapa Flow. Someone said it's in Scotland."

"It's in the Orkneys."

Velma hadn't noticed Tom and Josie were visiting. Tom knew more than she did so she sat down to question him.

"What damage did they do, Tom? How bad is it? I hope too many people didn't get killed."

"There's not been much released about it yet. The Germans apparently bombed the Navy's place in Scapa Flow. I went there once years ago. It's a pretty little place. You pass it as you go over on the ferry to the Orkneys."

"Tom, that's part of Britain. I didn't think they could get so close." Josie twisted her hands. "Does this mean that horrible Hitler man can attack the rest of the country?"

"Don't you worry, Josie." Tom patted his wife's hand. "Hitler will have to get past all the artillery waiting for him before he can set foot on these shores."

Velma and Florence smiled wistfully at one another. How lovely to see Tom reassure his wife. Both Mrs. Stanleys wished their husbands could be there with them.

The Germans got a step closer each week. The government introduced more rationing. May 1940 arrived and Hitler's army reached France. Velma worried about Jack's safety. She knew his company moved around Northern France, but not the exact location.

*Florence is so lucky. She knows George is still in a camp in England, even if she doesn't know the exact place.* Velma worried about Jack so much. She tried not to let this show in her letters. He had enough to cope with without having to worry about her, too.

When the Germans destroyed Middlesborough the sisters joined the horrified disbelief of the rest of Britain. Suddenly, the war sat on their doorstep.

A few days later they heard a new Prime Minister had been appointed -- Mr. Winston Churchill.

"Do you think this new man will make any difference?" Velma longed for the change to bring Jack home sooner. She knew how little chance her wish had of coming true.

"I don't know, Velma. We just have to go on day by day to make sure the world we know survives for the next generation. My Sam, for instance." Florence looked fondly at her son who sat at the dining room table colouring a picture to send to his daddy.

"I just feel so helpless. I wish I could do something more to help the war effort."

"You're not thinking of going to work on the land or in one of the armament factories are you?" Florence's horrified expression brought a smile to Velma's lips. In times of war everyone did the best they could. The old levels of acceptability and non-acceptability had changed. "I don't think Jack would like that. They get all sorts working there."

"I haven't really decided. But I have to do something."

*I don't want any old job. I want something that links me to Jack, if only in my heart.*

"I know how you feel. I'm going to apply to the post office when Sam starts school in September. Even if I can only work part-time it will release someone to do more essential work."

Velma had to suppress a grin at the expression on Florence's face. Her sister's apprehension appeared obvious. Did she think Velma would laugh at her statement?

"Good for you." She hugged Florence and went to see if she could help Sam.

*****

Velma arrived home from work one day in the middle of May feeling in low spirits. It had been a hard day and she hadn't heard from Jack for several weeks. She knew the mail had probably been delayed, but it didn't stop her worrying.

"Any mail, Florence?"

"Shhh..."

Florence huddled beside the radio listening to the announcer's posh voice.

"...Admiralty have made an Order requesting all owners of self-propelled pleasure craft between 30' and 100' in length to send all particulars to the Admiralty within 14 days from today if they have not already been offered or requisitioned."

When it became obvious the programme had recommenced, Florence turned the radio off.

"What do you think it means?" Velma asked.

"I don't know. I sat listening to a music programme when suddenly they said an important announcement would be made and everyone should listen. Then that came on."

The next few days Velma knew something would happen soon. The radio request and no news from Jack set her nerves on edge. She wished she knew if it would be good or bad. How would Jack be affected? She could almost touch the tension building up in the community. She still hadn't had any letters from Jack and her worry increased. Tom told her they were fighting in Northern France. The silence might mean Jack had moved on. The last she'd heard he had been in the area of the fighting.

Her steps dragged as she made her weary way home from work one evening. Despite her aching feet Velma stopped when she caught sight of a poster in the window of the corner shop. A smart young woman in naval uniform saluted with the words "Women's Royal Navy Service" above her head. Below, in much larger letters, the words "Join the Wrens and free a man for the fleet" were emblazoned.

Could this be what she'd been looking for? She didn't think the Wrens actually fought, but they did useful work releasing sailors for duty at the front. Plus her father had been in the Navy, so this might be her way to help with the war. She'd mention it in her next letter to Jack -- if she ever heard from him.

Her head full of plans to find out about the Wrens, she entered Florence's kitchen. Her sister sat at the table, her face as white as a sheet.

"Florence, what's wrong? Has something happened to George?"

"No. As far as I know he's fine."

"Then what is it? Not Jack. Please don't say something's happened to Jack."

Velma's heart lurched, thudding in an attempt to break out of her chest. Fear gripped her as Florence rushed towards her.

"Velma, I don't know. Honestly. Do you remember the announcement about the small boats? The Government has requisitioned the boats. Tom came round to tell me he'd heard our troops were trapped on the beaches at some little place in France opposite Dover. The big ships can't get in close enough so they need all the small ones they can get to lift the troops off the beach and take them further out. That's all he knew."

"Jack. He's in France."

Velma felt the blood drain from of her face. Now she knew why Florence had looked so shocked. She put her hand on the back of a chair and sank shakily onto the seat. A litany pounded through her brain, over and over.

*Keep my Jack safe, let him come home to me -- keep my Jack safe, let him come home to me.*

# Chapter Twelve

*Early June 1940*

Gunfire, screaming engines, the sound of thousands of men pushed into too small a space, the noise incredible. Jack and Pete permanently disabled as many vehicles as they could. If it couldn't be destroyed by smashing it, they removed some vital part and placed it on a pile. Other soldiers collected the items and threw them as far out to sea as possible. Both men worked furiously finishing one vehicle and moving on to the next.

Nearer to the sea's edge, troops embarked on small boats to be taken out to the larger ships which were unable to come close to the beach due to the shallow draft. Laden ships departed in quick succession while other newly arrived vessels took their place. Jack glanced toward the sea. It reminded him of a swarm of ants fussing round their queens. He wiped his grubby sleeve across his forehead to remove the sweat, and turned back to the job at hand.

The chatter of machine gun sounded from the dunes above the beach and spurts of sand exploded near Jack and his friend. Both dived for cover. Jack felt a sting as a bullet found him. He could barely cope with the pain spreading out from the wound. The last thing he remembered Pete yelled, "Jack. Are you all right? Jack, have you been hit?"

*****

Days passed and Velma lived her life on automatic. She went to work, did her job efficiently, came home, played with Sam, ate the food in front of her and to all intents and purposes appeared to be her normal self. Inside her thoughts were a mess.

Her mind kept presenting her with the worst images of Jack wounded, trying to come home to her, unable to find the right way. The nights were worse when she shut her eyes and couldn't get rid of the images of Jack lying dead on the beaches of a foreign shore. The nights in her lonely bed were the only times she allowed herself to cry. Even then she stifled the sound in her pillow. She wondered if Florence heard her, but her sister never mentioned it, although she appeared concerned every morning.

Tom came round often to give them the news he'd heard of the events on the beaches of Dunkirk.

"They're getting our lads off as quickly as possible. The RAF is strafing the enemy gun emplacements and keeping their planes away. Velma, if you haven't heard then there's nothing to hear."

"Remember what Mum always said," Florence said, obviously forgetting for a moment Velma had never really known their mother. "No news is good news."

"You probably won't hear anything until Jack's back on English soil. Keep your chin up, Velma, it won't be long now."

Tom's words cheered her a little. She headed for work the next morning with a heavy heart. How much longer could she keep this up without breaking down completely?

Later in the morning she listlessly tidied underneath her counter and ignored the excited sounds in the distance. They appeared to be heading in her direction. She thought she heard someone call her name, decided she'd misheard and kept her head down. Not really interested in anything but her unhappy thoughts, she refused to take notice. When she heard Florence's voice she jerked her head up.

"Velma. Where are you?"

Her sister's voice rose almost to a shout. Velma jumped up, intending to tell her to keep the noise down. As soon as Florence caught sight of her she waved an envelope in the air.

Velma held her breath, hardly daring to exhale as Florence came closer.

*Please, please, please don't let it be a telegram to say Jack's dead.*

Hands shaking, she snatched the envelope from Florence. It didn't look like the ones received by those who had lost loved ones.

"Open it, quick!"

Like a step out of time Velma noticed Florence had come alone.

"Where's Sam?"

"Never mind about Sam. He's with Josie. She had come for a visit when the telegram arrived. Now, open it."

Velma had been trying to delay the moment of putting her finger under the flap and opening the flimsy envelope. The urge to open it flowed over her and she nearly ripped the envelope in her haste. The paper fell into her hands and she unfolded it and read the words printed on the official telegram notepaper.

"Oh."

"What do you mean 'oh'?" Florence demanded.

"He's all right. Jack's all right." Velma wanted to take her sister's hands and dance round the counter but suddenly remembered Mrs. Harris. She glanced around. Mrs. Harris stood nearby a concerned look on her face. She blinked in surprise. Her supervisor smiled at her.

"What does it say?"

Velma knew Florence needed to know for George's sake and Ma Stanley would have to know, too.

"The telegram is from Jack's friend Pete. *Jack hurt stop Fine now stop Home soon stop Pete.*"

Suddenly, the euphoria wore off and she read the telegram again.

"Florence you don't think this means Jack's been badly injured do you? Pete doesn't really give much information."

"Telegrams are expensive. I expect he said as much as he could afford."

"Mrs. Stanley, I think you should go home with your sister. You've had a shock and it would be best if you were with your family until you know the full details." Mrs. Harris gave her a pat on her shoulder. "Off you go my dear and get your coat. I'm sure your sister will wait for you."

Back home Velma sat and cradled the cup of tea Florence placed in her hands. The telegram lay on the table in front of her and she kept reading it over and over again, trying to decipher what Pete had meant by 'Jack hurt'.

"Why don't you go and have a lie down," Florence suggested. "You'll feel better if you have a rest. When you wake up you'll be able to look at things in a clearer light. No don't take the telegram with you. I'll put it up here out of Sam's way. Go on."

Velma allowed herself to be shooed up the stairs. She lay down on her bed and tried to relax. Every time she closed her eyes she could see Jack badly maimed or worse, missing some limbs. Eventually she gave up trying to sleep and lay quietly thinking of the man she loved.

She must have dozed without realising it. A little later she heard a commotion downstairs, but put it down to Sam being his usual boisterous self. She turned over and drifted back to sleep.

A hand stroking her cheek woke her. She could feel the weight of someone sitting on her bed and she peered through her lashes. She hoped the person would leave her alone if they thought she slept.

"I know you're awake, Velma. I can see your eyes sparkling through your lashes."

"Jack!" Velma shot up in the bed. Her heart pounded. His sudden appearance had been such a shock.

Jack pulled her into his arms and smothered her face with kisses.

"Velma, my darling, you don't know how good it is to see you again. I've missed you so much."

She hugged him tight, and then pushed him to arm's length.

"Are you all right, Jack? Pete sent a telegram. He said you'd been hurt."

"Pete's an idiot. I told him to say I'd recovered and would be home soon. When he told me what he meant to send, I asked him to take out the bit about being hurt. He said if I'd recovered you'd wonder why I hadn't sent the telegram myself."

"But you were hurt?"

"I got shot in the shoulder. Only a graze. It hurt like mad at first. Once they'd cleaned it up they could see it didn't look too bad. I got Pete to send the telegram. I didn't have time before I caught the train."

"I worried about you so much, Jack. Are you sure you're all right?" Velma needed his reassurance after the last few days of uncertainty and worry.

"Yes, I'm fine. Guess what? I've got several weeks leave so we can have a honeymoon."

"Really? What if I can't get the time off? Should we really take time for ourselves when things are so bad? Jack, I--"

"Stop right there, Velma." He tilted her chin up with his finger until she stared into his eyes. "There's nothing we can do about the war. I'll be doing my bit when I go back off leave. You're doing your bit by keeping things going at home. We're entitled to take time for ourselves. Time to put aside some memories to keep us warm on the long nights apart."

"Silly." Velma punched him gently in the shoulder. Jack winced. "Oh, Jack, I'm sorry. I forgot about your shoulder."

"It's nothing." He smiled at her. "Come here my love."

Velma moved closer and melted into his arms.

*****

"Jack, can I ask you something?" Velma lifted the sunglasses from her eyes and looked at her husband who sat in the deckchair next to her.

"You can ask me anything you like, sweetheart."

"I've been thinking about joining the Wrens. I'd like to do my bit for the war. Joining the Women's Navy means I can do just that."

"What does it involve?" Jack leaned forward a concerned expression on his face. "You won't be fighting, will you?"

"No, of course not." Velma patted his hand. She loved it when he got all protective. "I looked into it before we came away and the recruiting lady thinks I'd probably be put on board the *HMS Paris*. I might do deciphering or tracking. You know pushing little boats around to show where their positions are."

"Velma, my love, if it's what you want to do then go ahead. I know what you mean about doing your bit, and I'd be proud to be able to say my wife's a Wren." He smiled and reached over and kissed her. "Mmm, you're good enough to eat."

"Is that a signal my man wants his lunch? I must admit I'm hungry. Let's eat then go for a walk. Afterwards we could have a lie down before tea." She gave him a grin full of wicked temptation. Velma had at last got used to their afternoon lovemaking and knew she'd miss him a lot when he left.

"Come on then, lazybones." Jack dragged her to her feet. "I'll give you a hand with preparing the food."

They ate then set off across the fields. Velma would have loved to take her honeymoon at the seaside, but they couldn't do this. Due to the war all the beaches were closed. Instead they'd been offered a small caravan on a farm near Boveysand Cliffs, as close to the sea as they could get. Velma admitted to herself it didn't really matter where they were, as long as she and Jack were together. She knew their time alone would be all too short. Soon

Jack would return to the front and once again his life would be in danger.

Hand in hand they walked through the springy grass, avoiding the fields with crops or animals. The balmy air and clear blue sky made it pleasant, especially as warm sun shone down on them.

"This is heaven." Jack took in a deep draught of fresh air. "You'd hardly think they were fighting a war on the other side of the water."

He waved at the small amount of sea they could see on the horizon. Velma shuddered. She didn't like to be reminded of the war. One of the women she worked with had received a telegram from the War Office stating her husband had died. Velma remembered when she'd been waiting for news about Jack.

"Let's not think about the war, Jack. We've only got a few days left. Can't we enjoy them?"

"Of course, my love." He squeezed her arm. "I think it's time we returned for our afternoon nap, don't you?"

Velma laughed, all thoughts of the war forgotten as they turned and walked quickly back to the caravan.

*****

*Summer 1940*

They returned to Plymouth. Jack went back to camp but he returned a few weeks later for a long weekend. The summer weather of glorious sunshine had Velma thinking she could be forgiven for putting the war to the background. Families got together for picnics, pooling their rations to make things as festive as they could.

People relaxed and enjoyed themselves. The winter had been hard. Rations had made tempers, as well as food, short, especially when everything they'd considered essential couldn't be obtained. The news from the front had not been good, but the summer weather pushed that to the back of the mind for a short time. All too soon bad news arrived to shatter their good mood. London had been bombed.

*****

Jack and Velma spent another few days at the caravan and upon their return Florence met them with news of the bombing. Jack tightened his arm around Velma as her body tensed.

"Will you have to go back early?" Jack heard the concerned tremor in her.

"Not unless they send a telegram." Jack looked at Florence who shook her head. "They'll let me know if they want me. Let's just enjoy the last few days before I have to go."

He saw the worry on Velma's face although she tried to hide it. Josie had invited them round for tea that evening and he knew his wife didn't want to go. He hated to force her, but they couldn't be rude.

"Tom's out at the moment but he'll be back soon," Josie told them when they arrived. "Of course, he has to go out again when it gets dark. We'll have a few hours together." They'd just finished helping Josie lay the table when Tom arrived. He looked tired but he visibly brightened as he greeted Velma and Jack.

"It's good to see you two. Did you have a nice holiday?"

"Lovely, thank you." Velma kissed his cheek and hugged him. Jack smiled. Tom had been the nearest thing Velma had to a father and Jack knew of her fondness for the man.

"Sit. Sit," Josie ordered as she and Velma placed the food on the table. When they were all seated Josie beamed round the table at everyone. "Now isn't this nice? Just like old times."

For several minutes a comfortable silence reigned while they ate their meal. When they'd cleared away the crockery and made a hot drink, Tom decided the time had come to talk.

"Did you hear about London? The bombs?"

"Florence told us as soon as we arrived home. Do you know how bad they got hit?" Jack asked.

"Mainly the dock area from what we can find out. Mind you there are a lot of people live around the docks so it probably means there's been a tremendous loss of life. There are rumours the bombers will strike other places next." Tom's sombre expression told Jack the older man thought the planes might head for Plymouth.

When Velma and Josie disappeared into the scullery, he and Tom talked freely.

"So you think the bombs might fall here next?"

"I'm afraid so," Tom replied with an exasperated sigh. "We have the dockyard and the naval base. It's a definite temptation for the enemy."

"Do you think it will be bad?"

"I don't want to think about it." Tom shook his head. "I don't want to look for trouble before it arrives."

The four of them sat around talking about family, friends and the war in general. All too soon Tom had to leave to do his stint as a fire warden.

"I'll walk with you. I'll be back soon, Velma. You two ladies probably need time to chat to each other and I need some fresh air."

Jack dropped a kiss on the top of Velma's head and followed Tom from the room.

The two men walked in silence for a while. Jack eventually cleared his throat and turned to Tom.

"You don't have to ask, Jack," Tom told him. "Josie and I will take good care of Velma. At least as good as we can in these troubled times."

"Thank you. That means a lot to me." Jack offered his hand and Tom shook it with warm friendliness.

"My station is just around the corner," Tom told him. "You'd better get back before the women start worrying about you."

Jack turned to leave but a distant sound caught his attention. Slowly, he turned back to Tom.

"It's them, isn't it?"

Tom nodded then turned and ran towards his warden station. The air raid sirens suddenly shattered the silence. Jack quickly followed.

# Chapter Thirteen

"What's that?" Velma jumped from her chair and ran into the back yard.

"Velma. The blackout." Josie hurried to turn the lights off then joined Velma.

The two women stood in the darkness with their arms round one another. In the distance they heard the roar of planes getting nearer. The sirens erupted drowning out the engine drone.

"The shelter," Josie gasped. "We have to get to the shelter."

"No, I have to find Jack. Where is he? He can't be with Tom all this time."

"We'll look for him when the 'all clear' sounds. Velma be sensible. We must go to the shelter."

With dragging steps, Velma allowed herself to be taken by the arm and guided to the Anderson shelter buried in the garden. She remembered the men of the family going from one sister's house to the next, digging the holes and burying the shelters. Once they'd been kitted out with small cots and shelves they were quite cosy.

Josie shut the door behind them. At first Velma sat engrossed in thoughts of Jack, wondering about his safety. Each night Josie poured hot water into a Thermos flask in case they had to go to the shelter. She'd just done this when the siren sounded. Now she offered Velma a cup of cocoa. Velma hugged it between her hands and looked around her. Josie and Tom had really made this place comfortable. There were a couple of deckchairs and two cots, plus tins of food and a tin opener on the shelf. A Tilley lamp and two torches provided light with several candles and a box of matches as a standby.

"What's that?" Josie's voice trembled.

Both women tilted their heads as they heard a rumbling in the distance. Gradually the noise became louder.

"It's the Germans." Josie's face drained of blood. Frightened by the noise, she couldn't stop a tremor going through her body.

"Don't worry, Josie, they're headed for the dockyard. We'll be fine."

A voice in Velma's head asked how she knew that. Even if they were fine, what about Jack and Tom? The men were out there. Were they in a shelter? She felt dizzy and sick thinking of Jack at the mercy of the German bombs.

The corrugated iron walls of the shelter closed in on her, and she longed to throw herself through the door and scramble up the steps to the back garden. Only Josie's presence prevented her. Her mild claustrophobia became worse with the sound of the huge engines on the enemy planes. They were right overhead now.

Her friends were of the opinion you never heard the bomb that hit you, but this didn't provide any consolation. The noisy throbbing? They might not hear the one that hit them, but what if the bomb landed on Jack and Tom? Both she and Josie heard the noise at the same time. A piercing whistle grew louder until it screamed like a very angry boiling kettle. It passed right overhead and moments later the ground shook violently. The sisters hugged one another in fear and they stayed this way until the 'all clear' sounded forty-five minutes later. Several more shocks had rocked their safe haven. Apart from a few tins falling off the shelf they were unscathed.

"Shall we see if the house is still there?" Josie hesitated.

"I'll go first, shall I?"

Velma longed to get out of this tin coffin and she flung the door open and climbed the few steps to ground level. The house stood solemnly in darkness. They'd turned off all the lights and drawn the blackouts before heading for the shelter.

"It looks fine, Josie. You stay there for a moment while I take a closer look."

Velma walked towards the house and cursed as she stubbed her toe on something hard in the grass. She found a few more obstacles with her feet then reached the back door and cautiously opened it. The torch in her hand wavered back and fro across the kitchen. A few items had fallen to the floor; otherwise she could see no damage.

"Is it all right?" Velma jumped as Josie spoke and peered over her shoulder at the same time. "Oh good, they missed us."

"I'm going to search for Jack."

Velma headed determinedly for the front door.

"He'll come back here," Josie said. "Wait for him to come home, Velma."

"Jack will be helping Tom." She knew her man. He wouldn't come home while he could help. "Make a flask of tea and I'll go look for them."

Josie bustled about and presently handed Velma a Thermos full of weak tea. She peered at her little sister and shook her head, then pulled Velma into a hug.

"You be careful, and if you can't find them -- come back here."

"I will. I promise."

Velma could hardly believe the streets were in the same town. Tom's watch point only stood a few corners away and it usually took her about five minutes to get there. Tonight she took a lot longer. The roads were blocked with rubble of collapsed buildings and fires lit things with an eerie, flickering glow. Occasionally, she ducked as an explosion came from nearby fires.

She found her way blocked by a huge blaze before she got as far as the Warden's shelter. A crowd stood watching as the fire wardens tried to put it out. They were helped by several women who passed water buckets down a line.

"Jack!"

The word exploded from her lips, but sounded no louder than a whisper. She could see him working beside Tom, flames licking around their bodies. Velma ran forward. If Jack stood helping to fight the fire then she needed to take her place beside him.

*****

Upon reaching the warden's station Jack and Tom settled down to wait out the air raid. The 'all clear' sounded and the wardens headed out to assess the damage and see what needed to be done.

They passed the rubble of a collapsed building that had received a direct hit. Some of the wardens left the main group to fight the small outbreaks of fire flickering in the ruins. The main body passed down the street and turned the corner. The scene in front of Jack convinced him he'd walked into hell.

Flames erupted from the bottom of a building. The stone front had peeled away opening up a view of the rooms inside. Jack noticed absurd things. A wardrobe hovering at the edge of the bedroom floor, the bed nudging against it. Both pieces of furniture threatened to topple onto the rubble beneath.

The fallen stone of the broken building hid the ground floor while massive flames greedily attacked the rest of the house. The blazing inferno jumped and roared fed by household items falling from inside the open rooms.

Tom called to the nearby spectators to form a bucket chain and the wardens sent one of their own to alert the fire service while they attacked the flames. Minutes later Jack could see why the wardens wore black. His own uniform showed soot stains and sweat poured from every part of him. Each time he wiped his brow with the back of his hand, it came away streaked with soot. The wardens brought the area of fire in front of him under control so he straightened and wiped his forehead again. He looked around. To his surprise a number of men stood watching the fire fighters, while several women joined the bucket chain, cheering one another on.

"Lazy devils," Jack muttered. He couldn't understand how the men could stand by and watch a building burn without offering any help, especially when the women were showing them up by helping the wardens.

He returned to the fray throwing buckets of water onto the heart of the flames. He glanced sideways when something beside him moved.

"Velma, what are you doing here?"

"Helping you." She grinned at him, her white teeth startling against her soot streaked face. "Someone has to make sure you're not hurt."

At that moment the fire brigade arrived and the helpers moved back to allow the trained men and women to do their work.

Jack put his arm around Velma and kissed the top of her head. Tom joined them and they watched as the fire dwindled to a smouldering heap.

"Tom, why didn't those men help us fight the fire?" Jack still couldn't believe the men had stood and watched the women doing the job they should have done.

"Most of them are in reserved jobs," Tom replied. "I'm not sure if they think fighting fires is beneath them or if there's another reason. Lucky the women don't feel the same way."

Jack shook his head. The logic of some people had to be beyond him.

"We've had word there's been a lot of damage, but there weren't many fires."

"That's good, Tom." Jack clapped him on the back. "I could do with a cuppa now, couldn't you?"

"Oh, I almost forgot." Velma rummaged in her coat and Jack wondered what on earth she could be doing. "Here we are. Josie sent a flask of tea."

As she flourished the flask it slipped from her fingers and Jack neatly scooped it out of the air before it hit the ground.

"Let's leave this with Tom," he suggested. "I don't know about you but I'm dead beat. I need a nice long sleep."

Jack and Velma walked to Josie's first to let her know Tom had suffered no hurt. Then they continued on to Florence's.

They used the scullery to wash the residue of the fire from their bodies, then went upstairs and slipped between the sheets. Jack took Velma into his arms and pulled her close.

"You know how much I love you, don't you my darling?"

"And I love you too, my Jack. I'm going to be so lonely without you."

"I know, my love. Once this war's over I'm never going to leave you again."

Jack's lips brushed Velma's and the kiss deepened as Velma's arms snaked around his neck. He couldn't believe he'd won this wonderful woman. Out of all his sisters-in-law he'd always liked Florence the best. He'd never guessed she had such a beautiful sister. They were nothing alike in personality, although they shared a slight similarity in their noses and eyes. He took one more moment to look at the woman who had given herself to him, and then he lost himself in her body.

*****

Jack returned to the war and for a few days Velma's unhappiness showed on her face.

"Misery feeds on misery," Florence told her. "Cheer up and you'll find things aren't as bad as you think."

Velma knew her sister talked sense. She decided to go ahead with her plans to join the Wrens, but didn't say anything to her family. If she didn't get in they wouldn't need to know anything about her attempt.

"Why do you wish to join the Woman's Royal Navy?" The recruiting officer stared intently at Velma, who quaked in her shoes.

"My husband is in the services," she stammered. "And I'd like to do my bit. Plymouth is a naval town so it only seems right to apply to join the Navy."

"Have you been married long?"

"A year. I'm living with my sister while my husband is overseas. Her husband is also away so we're company for one another."

"Your forms are in order, Mrs. Stanley. As long as you pass the physical we'll be happy to accept you into the Navy." The woman smiled and held out her hand. "Congratulations. We could do with more women like you helping with the war effort."

Velma still didn't say anything to the family. She went for the physical and passed with flying colours. Now she had to break the news. Hopefully, they'd take it well, but she didn't really know how the family would react. She decided to wait until Sunday. Despite the rationing the sisters tried to hold afternoon tea once a month at Josie's.

The table looked bare. The only cakes or sweet things were reserved for the children. The adults made do with salad grown in their own garden, and the small bits of cheese they could spare. Velma waited until they'd eaten. The children were playing in the garden while their mothers enjoyed a weak, but well-earned, cup of tea. She cleared her throat to catch their attention.

"I've got some news." She paused and before she could continue Enid spoke.

"You're not pregnant, I hope. This is not the time to bring a child into the world."

"No, I'm not having a baby. I've joined the Wrens."

A hubbub of noise met this announcement as all the sisters tried to speak at once.

"You've done what?"

"Don't be silly. You can't..."

"Velma, that's wonderful."

"Does Jack know?"

The last from Enid. Her voice made it evident she didn't think Velma had told her husband about this bit of madness.

"Of course Jack knows. At least he knows I intended to try and join the Wrens. I've written to tell him I've been accepted."

"Well, I think it's wonderful." Florence glared at Enid, daring her to say anything nasty. "I suppose this means you'll be moving out."

"Only while I'm training. I'll be able to come home on my days off."

"How long does it take to train you?" Tears rushed to Josie's eyes.

"They said about three months."

"When do you go?" This from Florence whose expression flicked from pleased to downhearted. Velma smiled apologetically at her. Poor Florence would be on her own with Sam.

"At the end of the week. I gave in my notice at the store as soon as I knew I'd got in. I hope you're all happy for me. Every one of you is doing your bit taking care of the children and Red Cross and the like. I wanted to do war work. Serving in a shop is not much when there's so little to sell. Joining the Wrens means I'm fighting the enemy in my own way."

"Of course we're happy for you, aren't we girls?" This time Florence glared at all the sisters and they hurried to assure Velma they were very proud of her. Even Enid made a brusque but supportive comment.

"You're a good girl, Velma. Everyone should do their best in this war, and you're helping as you see fit."

*****

The following week a nervous Velma stood in line with the other new trainees and listened to the speech given by the Senior Wren. She longed to scratch the itch the uncomfortable uniform gave her as it rubbed her neck, but didn't want to attract the wrath of the Senior. Another woman had shuffled her feet and received an instant punishment. Velma forced herself to listen, afraid she might miss something important.

"Now you have your uniforms and know what is expected from you, Wren Jones will show you where you are to sleep. Don't forget Wrens, you are expected to be on parade by seven in the morning."

The junior Wren showed them to their bunkroom and left them to it.

"Phew! I thought I would be helping my country. The Senior Wren made it sound like I had been sent here to stop me posing a threat to England." The girl who'd spoken grinned at Velma. "I'm Lottie. Charlotte Beardsley really, but that's too posh for the likes of me."

"Velma Stanley. Pleased to meet you."

"Oh no. We can't have you called Velma, that's almost as bad as Charlotte. Have you got a middle name?"

"No sorry, I think my mum and dad ran out by the time they got to me. There are seven sisters and a brother older than me."

"Lucky you. I'm an only child. Sometimes spoilt, other times not allowed to do anything. Are you single or married?"

"Married. Jack's away with the army." Lottie's questions were a bit intrusive. Velma smiled. The woman had only tried to be friendly.

"Well, I guess I'll just have to get used to calling you Velma."

Velma breathed a sigh of relief at Lottie's decision. She would have found it hard to respond to anything but her given name.

A bell high on the wall rang and the new recruits left the bunk room to make their way to mess hall. When they'd eaten Lottie wanted to go for a walk, but Velma declined. She had to take whatever spare time she could find to write to Jack. Today she wanted to let him know about her first day as a Wren.

*My darling Jack*

She stopped, then sucked the end of her pen. Where should she start? Probably from when she left Florence's.

*Today I joined up, you know what I joined. Florence and Sam walked me to the bus stop and there were tears when the bus came. I stood on the platform waving until I couldn't see them anymore.*

*At the gates of the base they checked I hadn't brought in anything I shouldn't. Luckily there were several women officers to check through the suitcase. There were lots of women recruits and we got issued with our uniforms and taken through the base to familiarise ourselves with where we're allowed to go and the places that are forbidden. The senior officer gave us a talk on how we should behave, what we would be expected to learn and how we must obey senior officers at all times.*

*I think I've made a friend...*

# Chapter Fourteen

*...her name is Lottie, really Charlotte but she doesn't like that name. She wanted to make up a nickname for me. She couldn't think of one, thank goodness.*

*Everyone at home is fine. I had a letter from your mother the other day and she seems to be holding up well. Your brother Will is there to help if she needs anything, but you know how most people feel nowadays.*

The letter finished with Velma declaring her love and how much she missed him. Jack smiled as he put the page back into the envelope and tucked it in his tunic. He liked the idea of Velma doing something for the war effort. He knew she hated the war, most women did. Unfortunately, if they wanted to live and bring up their children with freedom of choice it had to be done. He and Velma had to fight for their country's right to be free.

"Letter from the Missis, Jack?" Pete thumped him on the shoulder.

"Yep. She's joined the Wrens," Jack stated proudly.

"Good for her. You married a good one there, mate."

Jack grinned and returned to cleaning the spark plugs of the lorry he repaired. Pete settled in for a chat as he sat down on a nearby oil drum.

"Have you heard the rumour we won't be going home for Christmas?"

"Didn't really expect to, did you, Pete? We're in a war, not a church picnic."

"I know. I sort of hoped we might make it home this year. I haven't spent Christmas with my mum for years. There might not be another chance what with her getting old and me out here."

"Stop being so morbid. Talk like that will get you down and make you careless. When's your mum's birthday?"

"March. Think I'll write and tell her I probably won't be home before then, so we'll have a big party for her birthday when I get there." Pete had already cheered up a bit and Jack smiled.

"Good for you. Maybe you'll be able to pick up something nice for her over here."

Pete wandered off a more cheerful expression on his face than when he arrived. Jack shook his head and turned back to the lorry engine. His hands worked automatically to repair the damage but his thoughts returned to Velma.

How would his lovely bride manage in the rough and tumble of navy life? Or did the women's section of the Navy provide such a rough and ready life as the men's side? Probably not. They'd still be expected to uphold the dignity and tradition of the service. Velma had been used to having any problems sorted out for her. Even though she tried to stand on her own two feet, her sisters had a habit of stepping in and protecting her.

Jack shook his head. Although he worried about Velma, he could do nothing about it. He could only try to stay safe and return home to her in one piece.

The following day his thoughts returned to haunt him. The RASC tended to be near the back of the lines, proving support and transport for those in the thick of the fighting. Unfortunately, the lines wavered and Jack's corps found themselves surrounded by fighting men, their own and the enemy. Someone thrust a rifle into his hand and told him to return fire.

The RASC men had all received basic training with guns, but Jack had never actually shot at anyone. He hesitated. A soldier wearing enemy uniform pointed his rifle in his direction. Jack let instinct take over. The gun in his hand sprang up and his finger pulled the trigger. The soldier dropped his weapon and fell to the ground, his hand clasped to his shoulder.

At that moment reinforcements arrived and the battlefront moved away from their region. Jack found himself shaking with reaction for what he'd done.

*Thank God I didn't kill him.*

He knew he shouldn't be thinking of the Germans in this way. He'd never seen the enemy so close before. The soldier had been about his age, probably with a wife at home. How could he kill someone whose life probably mirrored his own?

"Well done, mate." Pete slapped him on the back. "You got that one good, didn't you?"

Jack tried to smile and shrug off Pete's praise. His friend wouldn't understand even if he tried to explain. Then he did smile. Velma would understand. She'd know his exact feelings.

What was she doing right now? Probably pushing the little boats around on the table in the Naval Base operation room or on *HMS Paris* doing something equally important.

*****

*March 1941*

Music hall tunes flowed from the radio and Florence picked up her knitting. Velma couldn't decide whether to do her sewing or write to Jack. Now she had completed her training she could come home on her days off.

"I heard something interesting today." Florence reached the end of a knit row and turned the needles round for the purl row. "There's a rumour the King and Queen are going to visit on Thursday to cheer up the boys in the Marine and Navy Barracks."

"Do you think it's true?"

"I know their majesties like to make unexpected visits to keep the morale up. It could be true. I'd love to take Sam to see them. I'm not sure whether they'll come into the city and in any case he'll be at school."

"Maybe I'll see them when I'm working. I hope you and Sam get a look at them."

Rumours flew round the base over the next few days. Velma wrote to Jack telling him Mum and Dad would probably visit sometime over the next few days. She hoped he would guess what she meant. Thursday morning she arrived at *HMS Paris* and Lottie pounced on her.

"Have you heard? Their majesties are coming here today. They're arriving by train this morning."

"Shh, Lottie. You know we've been told to be careful about what we say." Velma didn't think they were at risk but you could never be sure. Posters everywhere warned 'Loose lips sink ships' so for their fighting men's sake she tried to follow the maxim.

"But wouldn't it be exciting." Lottie lowered her voice to a whisper. "How often do we get the chance to see the King and Queen?"

"We'll be lucky if we see them this time, silly. They're coming to see the men, not us. Unless they want to see us pushing models and bits of paper around, it will be work as usual."

Murmurs flew round the operations room all morning until just before lunch an excited Wren confirmed their Majesties were on the base. Velma wouldn't be able to see the royal visitors, she had work to do. They were extremely busy this morning and she hurried from one job to another.

By the end of her watch Velma could honestly say she didn't want to hear another thing about the royal party. To be told they'd been here, done this or done that, when she had to stay in the operations room stretched her nerves to the limit. She had tomorrow off and decided to walk home and clear her head of the stuffiness of being in a ship all day. She'd reached the turnoff for the street where Florence lived, when a posh car with a police escort passed her, heading towards town. Velma recognised Queen Elizabeth in the rear seat. Her Majesty looked out the window and to her surprise nodded to her. Velma, still in uniform, straightened up and saluted smartly.

The car drove out of sight and Velma hurried home. She'd no sooner got in the door than Sam threw himself at her.

"Sam, you're really going to have to stop doing that," she gasped as she tried to get her breath back. "You're getting too big to jump on me."

"Aunty Vee, Aunty Vee. We saw the King and Queen -- twice."

"Did you? When? Tell me all about it."

Velma took off her hat and jacket and followed Sam into the kitchen. He chattered away about being on his way home from school with Aunt Josie when the royal car had passed them.

"She waved to me, Aunty Vee. The Queen waved to me."

"You're a very lucky boy," Velma told the six-year-old. She didn't want to burst his bubble by telling him the Queen had also waved at her. A big event for him at his age, why not let him have all the glory?

"Yes, he is. He also saw them at school. The teachers took all the children out to the playground beside the road when they heard their majesties were going to the naval base." Florence put the teapot and cups on the table. "Poor old mummy didn't get to see the royals and neither did Aunty Vee."

"Maybe next time." Sam sounded so grown up when he spoke. The women clutched their teacups to their mouths to hide their smiles.

Sam wandered off to play with his toy cars and Florence watched him fondly.

"He's growing so fast. I hope George doesn't miss too much of his childhood. How did your day go?"

"Same as usual. Oh, yes," Velma looked furtively behind her to make sure Sam had gone. "And the King and Queen drove past me on the way home. Her Majesty waved to me. I saluted her as a good Wren should."

"Thanks for not telling Sam. He's so proud the Queen waved especially to him."

"So how did your day go?"

"Not too bad. There's loads of mail coming through. I'm really glad I'm not in telegrams though. I'd hate to have to read all those condolences and to deliver them to the families would be even worse. At least all I have to do is sort the mail into the right boxes."

Florence had taken a job at the post office several months ago when Sam had settled into school. She loved being out of the house during the daytime as she found it lonely on her own. Josie obliged by taking and collecting Sam when Florence's shifts prevented her from doing so.

"There's some letters from Jack behind the tea caddy."

Velma jumped up from her seat and grabbed them. With a grin to Florence she hurried to her room to read them in private.

The censor had blacked out about half of each of the letters. From what remained she gathered Jack had been in some sort of skirmish. He made light of it, but she could tell by the way he wrote that he'd been shaken by the event. His last letter brought a smile to her lips.

*I am so proud of you my love. To know that you've joined up makes me feel humble that even the women of England are fighting back. Well done, my darling Velma, when this is all over we will be able to look back with pride on what we have achieved.*

The censors obviously thought this to be encouragement and not contravening any 'loose talk' so the whole paragraph had survived unscathed. She couldn't see anything about him coming home on leave soon, but that would have been cut out anyway. Maybe it wouldn't be too long.

She didn't even know his whereabouts at the moment. He might be in France again, or somewhere else.

During the next month there were times when she found it hard to believe the truth of a war being fought across the channel. Then the air raid sirens would scream out and the sound of planes were heard high above. They had no time to become complacent and both the women and men in England did their utmost to support the men overseas.

Velma went to *HMS Paris* each day, and sometimes worked the night shift, the time when most attacks occurred. Early in April she arrived for day shift and took her place in the ops room ready to collate the information as it arrived. Sometimes they went for hours with only a dribble of data, whereas at other times they were hard pushed to keep up with the flow.

This morning messages slowly trickled in, but soon they knew the day would be different. Messages arrived with increasing speed, telling of waves of enemy planes heading across the channel. At first Velma tried not to show her concern for the poor people who would suffer from this attack. Horrified, she saw the planes were heading for Plymouth. Their ship lay alongside the naval base right next to the dockyard. Her legs shook as it occurred to her the ship along with the ops room might become a target.

She wondered how it affected Jack when the planes flew over his position. Probably very much like she did now. They heard the crumpling sound of bombs hitting Plymouth. The noise came from the direction of the city centre and she hoped Florence, Sam and the rest of her family were safe in the shelters. Gradually the noise came closer until the planes droned right overhead. Bombs rained down causing the ship to buck and sway with the shift of land and sea. Velma almost fell but managed to keep herself upright by holding on to one of the sorting tables.

The attack went on forever and she had doubts they would survive. The tremendous noise along with the shaking and falling of things from shelves and tables, made the place look a shambles. Gradually the noise decreased and the senior officers gave orders to straighten the room. By the time they'd finished the 'all clear' sounded.

"At least we're alive." Lottie brushed the dust from the shoulders of her uniform. "Wouldn't want to go through another one like that though."

Velma agreed. She had a sinking feeling this would only be the beginning. Plymouth had not been badly hit before, but the Germans must be aware of the dockyard, an obvious target for their bombers.

Velma hated being right. Including the initial raid the bombers struck three times over the next few weeks. They'd thought this bad enough until they realised these attacks had been the prelude to the enemy's real offensive.

Every night the bombers ripped apart the night skies of Plymouth. Rains of bombs fell on the dockyard and naval base. Some also went astray over the city. Velma knew it didn't matter where she might be, a bomb always managed to fall nearby. Thankfully, none of the family experienced a direct hit. They mainly suffered from shock and nerves.

A brief respite made everyone hope Hitler had finished pummelling Plymouth. It was no to be. A few days later the planes arrived again. On duty this time, Velma became convinced she would not survive this second attack on the *HMS Paris*. The ops room lay far too close to the centre of the action and every night they survived they deemed to be a miracle.

At last the main barrage finished. Plymouth heaved a collective sigh of relief and Velma wrote to Jack. She told him the blitz, as it had been nicknamed, only made people more determined to win the war against the Germans. Several days later her commanding officer called Velma and Lottie into her office.

"Wrens, as you know we are operating at low level at the moment due to the recent attacks. Liverpool has asked for extra staff to help them due to the Irish Sea as well as the Atlantic on their doorstep. I am therefore transferring you to Liverpool for the next few months. You will return here when we become fully operational again."

A mixture of excitement and hesitancy swirled through Velma's mind. She'd never been further north than Bristol. Living in another port would be an adventure.

"Excuse me ma'am. When are we to leave?" She would need to warn Florence and write to Jack.

"Tonight, Wren Stanley. You have leave to return to your home and collect any items you feel you might need. I hope I don't have to tell you not to inform your family of your destination." The senior Wren's gimlet eyes glared at Lottie and Velma.

"No ma'am," they both hastily replied.

"Isn't it exciting?" Lottie tucked her arm through Velma's. "Off to Liverpool all on our own."

"Hardly on our own," Velma laughed. "There will be more Wrens in Liverpool than there are down here. And no doubt we're not the only ones travelling up there tonight."

She hurried home to tell Florence about her transfer to another base and to write to Jack.

*...So you see Jack, I'll be going away with Jenny for a few weeks, maybe longer. Her family lives near a pool so no doubt we'll get some swimming in before we have to come back. It will be nice and peaceful after the noisy nights we've had recently...*

Her clever Jack would work out what she meant. 'Jenny Wrens' were the affectionate term given to the ladies of the Royal Navy and the reference to the pool would instantly tell him where she'd been transferred. The 'noisy nights' might not get through the censors. She decided it to be worth a try.

"You take care now," Florence warned her as she stood with her suitcase at the front door. "I don't want to have to explain to Jack why I couldn't keep you safe."

"Florence, you couldn't possibly do anything with you down here and me in a different city." Just in time she'd stopped herself telling Florence her destination. Telling Jack in code stretched the limit. Her sister might innocently mention it and word could get back to the Senior Wren. Seeing the tears rush to her sister's eyes, Velma quickly gave her and Sam a hug and picked up her case.

"Don't worry, Florence, I'll be fine. I'll write to you when I get there."

With a final ruffle of Sam's hair she walked off down the road, heading for the station. She reached the corner and turned to wave one last time before the buildings blocked her view.

The journey to Liverpool on a darkened train left them bored and tired. The excitement at the beginning of the journey soon evaporated as the miles went slowly by. Every few minutes they had to stop to let a troop train go the other way. In reality Velma knew the stopping times were no more than one an hour. The train took all night to get to Merseyside and Velma and Lottie were relieved when they steamed into Liverpool Station.

"Well, here we are." Lottie smiled at a passing sailor. "What shall we do now?"

"Make sure we're neat and tidy and head for that grim looking lady at the end of the platform."

Velma had seen an older woman in Wrens uniform standing the other side of the ticket barrier and guessed the officer had come to meet them.

"There goes any fun we might have had before getting to the barracks." Lottie complained in a good natured way as they headed for the barrier. "Do you realise it's the first of May today? At least we'll get a good night's sleep for once."

Velma remembered her friend's words that night as she experienced a repeat of the nightly attacks on Plymouth. And it didn't stop at a few nights, the bombs dropped heavily for nearly a week.

She wrote to Jack later.

*I truly believe the horrible man across the water has got it in for me. He seems to follow me wherever I go. Nasty, noisy old man.*

She grinned as she read the words on the paper. She really believed Hitler to be a nasty, noisy old man. He not only kept her and Jack apart, he'd also dropped bombs on her. Velma wondered if the leader of Germany had made this war a personal vendetta against her.

She didn't know how long they'd be in Liverpool so she'd suggested Jack write to the British Forces Post Office instead of Florence's address. They'd never communicated this way before so she had no idea how long letters would take to come through. She hoped her beloved husband kept safe and thought of her often.

# Chapter Fifteen

*June 1942*

The sun beat down and Jack's clothes dripped with perspiration. He hadn't expected to be fighting in North Africa and had no way of letting Velma know his location. Even a mention of the heat would be sliced out by the censors. He scratched the dark stubble on his chin. Desert fighting meant little water, certainly not enough for shaving.

The last year had been packed with movement. Plus, there'd been the added worry of Velma being caught up first in the blitz of Plymouth and then immediately after with Liverpool and their blitz. He smiled as he remembered her letter complaining she thought Hitler had been targeting her personally. Her letters gave him a better understanding of her feelings when she worried about him. His company had been sent to Palestine, and then on to North Africa. He didn't much care for the dust and heat of Africa, and Palestine hadn't been much better.

"What do you think will happen, Jack?" Pete broke into his thoughts.

"I think the Germans will attack again. They've already got Tobruk. Stands to reason they'll want El Alamein, too. The bloke who's leading them seems to know what he's doing. Looks like he has unlimited men and supplies." Jack chewed the inside of his cheek as he thought about the possibilities for the British Armed Forces.

"Don't think we'll get reinforcements," Pete scuffed his feet on the sandy ground. He evidently didn't like the idea of continuing with their current numbers. "Too much fighting going on the other side of the Mediterranean. Our lot must be spread pretty thin by now."

"You're forgetting the Yanks. They're with us now. Maybe they'll come to North Africa to help."

Pete snorted and Jack took this to mean his friend didn't think much of the likelihood of this happening.

A few days later, Jack's words came true when the Germans fought around El Alamein. His company joined the rest of the army as they were pushed further and further back from their original positions. A month later they received some good news, and Jack wrote to Velma hoping she'd understand his words.

*My darling Velma,*

*It's good to know you're safe and well. Pete and I have been trying to get a suntan now the rain has stopped.*

Would she understand he had tried to tell her he'd left Europe and had now moved to the other side of the Mediterranean?

*Had some good news the other day. Uncle Monty has gone to stay with the family. Hopefully, he'll decide to be with them for a long time. They certainly need his help.*

*I hear Uncle Sam is being a big help to your family. These older men certainly show their worth during these troubled times, don't they?*

*I miss you so much, my love, and can't wait until I hold you in my arms again. Unfortunately, I don't know when that will be. Remember I'm thinking of you always.*

*Your loving husband,*
*Jack*
*xxxx*

The arrival of General Montgomery turned the tide of their part of the war. The Germans retreated and by February of the next year it looked like Rommel would be defeated. Unfortunately, it took him another two or three months and the arrival of American reinforcements before Rommel accepted the inevitable and surrendered.

"Do you think they'll send us home now, Pete?"

"No chance, mate. They'll keep us here forever if they can. Won't take the chance of losing everything again."

*****

*September 1943*

"Aunty Vee, have you had any letters from Uncle Jack?"

Velma smiled at Sam. He had grown into a lovely boy and now proved a great help to his mother. He considered himself the man of the family until his father returned. Now Velma had returned from Liverpool she could to see the family more often.

"Yes, Sam, I have. His section of the army seems to be winning their part of the war."

"Where is he, Aunty Vee? Is he where they're dropping the bombs?"

Sam had a natural morbid curiosity like most boys his age. It didn't seem to occur to him if the bombs dropped near his uncle there might be danger of him being killed.

"If you mean Europe, no I don't think he is although I can't be sure."

Velma turned away from Sam. Relieved Jack no longer had to dodge the cold, wet weather of Europe she still worried about him. If she'd guessed correctly he now had heat to contend with. She shuddered. Hot or cold, he still woke each morning with the German army nearby.

"Homework young man," Florence scolded but with a smile to take the edge off her words. "Get it done now in case we have to go to the shelter tonight."

Sam disappeared to his bedroom. Velma and Florence sat at the kitchen table sharing a pot of precious tea.

"So where do you think Jack is?"

"I'm not sure," Velma replied. "I think he's in North Africa. It sounded like this area last time he wrote. He might have moved on now. God, I wish this war would be over."

"I know what you mean. We've had nothing but rations, air raids and our men away for so long it seems like it's always been like this."

"I'd love to start a family. If the war goes on for much longer it will be too late for Jack and me."

"Rubbish, you've got years ahead of you."

Velma sighed. The longing for a child surged inside her. She knew it would be wrong to bring a baby into a world at war. She couldn't do anything about getting pregnant anyway, not with Jack overseas.

Each night in the barracks, or when she stayed at home with Sam and Florence, Velma poured over the newspapers or listened to the wireless. The war in Europe appeared to be going against the Germans. Hopefully, this meant the fighting would soon be over. Letters from Jack became scarce. His last one mentioned something about moving on. Unfortunately, the censors had been overly strict and most of the letter had been blacked out. Could he be coming home? Maybe in time for Christmas.

For a long time she didn't get any mail from Jack and she worried something might have happened to him. She told herself she'd know if he'd been hurt or anything worse. No, she refused to even think the words. Deep inside her mind uncertainty reared its head. Would she really know if something had happened to Jack?

# Chapter Sixteen

*Christmas 1943*

"Come on, Jack, join in the fun."

"No thanks, Pete."

"This is the first time in years we've been able to have time off at Christmas, even if it is on a ship. Let's make the most of it. We'll be back in the thick of it as soon as we reach Burma."

"I know." Jack leaned back to enjoy the sea breeze. "I keep worrying about Velma and wondering if she's understood the clues I put in my letters. I never imaged we'd come out here after North Africa, so we didn't arrange anything to cover this."

"Your Velma is a clever little thing. She'll have worked it out. Come on, have some fun."

"Thanks all the same, I think I'll write her another letter." Thoughts of Velma filled his head. All the things they'd experienced together made her more dear to him with each passing day. So intense were his thoughts he could smell the lavender soap she loved to use.

"Are you listening to me? Why do you have to write now? You can't post them until we meet another ship or reach port."

"I know, but I have to get them all ready to go, don't I?"

Jack grinned at his friend and went to where he had stowed his kitbag. He'd retrieved his notepad and pen when the general alarm sounded.

"All hands to emergency stations. All hands to emergency stations. This is not a drill. This is not a drill."

Thoughts of Velma flew from his mind as he ran to join his mates in the main mess hall. The RASC personnel were non-combatants as the navy were in charge of the guns and torpedoes. They could only stand by and watch and listen.

"Who do you think it is?" Pete asked as he joined Jack. "Japs or Germans?"

"Probably Japs. We're a bit too far East for the Germans."

The ship shook as her big guns let loose and the soldiers became silent. Their fellow allies were fighting a real battle and they weren't able to help in the fight.

The enemy fired back and Jack knew the reason for the orders to strap everything down. The whole room shook and despite being stacked in special shelves, several tins fell off with a clatter. He also heard the sound of pots and pans falling to the floor in the nearby galley.

The engagement quickly concluded and the 'All personnel return to normal stations' announcement came over the ships loudspeakers. Jack breathed a sigh of relief. They only had a few more days until they arrived at their destination, hopefully there would be no more attacks before then.

*****

*June 1944*

"They're saying it won't be long now. The war will soon be over." Silently Velma prayed the rumours would be true.

"They've been saying the same thing since September 1939. I won't believe it until our men are safely home." Florence shook her head. "I never thought when I had Sam I would be bringing him into such a horrible world. I might have thought twice about having a child if I'd known."

"But then you wouldn't have had the pleasure of Sam. He's growing up into such a lovely lad. You and George should be very proud of him." Velma had a fondness for Sam and hoped when the war had finished, she and Jack would have a little boy just like him.

"I am, really. Bombs dropping all the time and worrying about George is not the way he should be growing up. He should be able to have fun with his friends, go fishing with his father, all the sorts of things boys get up to at his age."

"Maybe they're right this time and it will all be over soon."

Florence gave an unladylike snort and Velma grinned. Her sister thought the Allies should march into Berlin and give Hitler a good talking to. She believed the rest of Europe shouldn't stand for such nonsense from a jumped up little house painter.

The days slipped by with the occasional letter from Jack. She'd picked up from his clues he now served in the Far East. This lay on the other side of the world -- so far away. Never having left England, Velma couldn't imagine what another country would be like, especially one so hot and humid.

Summer arrived with mild weather. Velma had been working long hours in the build up for the allies to regain Europe. Referred to as D-Day, Velma knew this would be the breaking point of the war, but she couldn't tell any of her family about it. The information remained classified and top secret.

At last she had a day off.

"I'll collect Sam from school if you like," she offered as Florence rushed out the door to work.

"Heavens, Velma, Sam's a big boy now. If you turned up at the school gates he'd be so embarrassed he wouldn't speak to you for a week." Florence laughed. "Why don't you meet me from work and we'll wait for him at the end of the road. Then we can all walk round to Josie's for tea. She's been complaining she doesn't see enough of us. George will be home for his weekend leave early tomorrow so we don't want to be too late tonight."

Velma agreed. She spent the day writing to Jack and tidying the house for Florence. She left in plenty of time to meet her sister and strolled along dreaming of what life would be like when Jack returned and they could begin married life properly.

*I really feel I've grown up during this awful war. If Jack asked me to live on Hayling Island I wouldn't hesitate for a second. It no longer matters if I'm not near my family. My sisters are family, but Jack is my reason for living.*

Dreams of a small house with Jack coming home from work each day to find her dishing up the evening meal. A deep happy sigh escaped her lips. A van careered past, disturbing her reverie.

Velma realised she'd almost reached Florence's workplace. The van rounded the last corner only seconds ahead of her. Velma shook her head at the reckless speedster. She turned the corner and saw Florence talking to a group of friends. Her sister turned at the sound of the van, and waved when she caught sight of Velma. Then everything happened in slow motion.

The van, still going far too fast, lost control and swerved towards the group of women. Velma opened her mouth to scream. Her voice stuck in her throat. She watched helplessly as the van left the road and somersaulted over and over. It landed directly where the women had been standing and slid towards the nearby building, ending against the wall with a sickening crunch.

For a moment, Velma stood frozen to the spot, then she ran. Several women were helped to their feet by others who had seen the horrifying accident. Velma couldn't see Florence anywhere. She prayed her sister had been hidden by the dust the accident had kicked up.

"Joan, where are you?"

Velma heard the terror shake the voice as an older woman frantically pulled the rubble of the fallen wall away from the van. She assumed the unknown Joan to be trapped under the debris with Florence. With the brick dust and the steam escaping from the destroyed radiator, Velma had difficulty seeing much.

Sirens split the shocked silence as the police and fire engines hurried towards the crash site. Velma didn't know what to do. She still couldn't see any sign of Florence and moved hesitantly round the crashed vehicle trying to see if her sister had been hidden by the van.

"Now then, love, come out of there and let us do our work."

A fireman took her by the arm and pulled her gently back.

"My sister, she stood with the other women. She..."

Velma couldn't continue. The fireman guessed what she had been trying to say.

"We'll see if we can find her. You stand over there with the others."

Velma stood beside the group of women on one side of the police car. She had no idea how she'd got there.

Several ambulance women had arrived and were treating those with superficial wounds. Nobody appeared to be badly hurt, but she couldn't see Florence. Apparently, Joan had also gone missing. The older woman who had been searching for her stood sobbing quietly into her handkerchief.

Velma clenched and unclenched her hands. They moved of their own accord, first moving spasmodically, and then twisting nervously around one another. She could see everything around as if from a distance. She must be dreaming. This couldn't be happening. Velma clung to the hope the firemen would find Florence beneath the rubble. Hurt but alive. How could she tell the family if Florence hadn't survived? She took deep breaths to still her churning stomach and straightened her shoulders. She wouldn't let her thoughts drift in that direction. Of course her sister would live.

Two firemen appeared from behind the van, one either side of a staggering figure, supporting her. Florence? Could it be her? Velma held her breath.

"Joan, oh Joanie you're alive." The sobbing older woman rushed forward to hug the dishevelled figure and Velma's heart dropped. Not Florence then.

The firemen handed their load over to the ambulance ladies and turned back to the crash site.

The next time they appeared they carried a body between them. A very still body. The head tilted to one side, allowing the auburn hair to fall over the face.

"Nooo."

Who made that horrible noise? Calling out like a banshee? The sound came from her own mouth. Weakness attacked her knees as she staggered forward.

Gently, the men laid the body on the stretcher the ambulance ladies had prepared. Velma fell to her knees and brushed Florence's hair away from her face. Blood mingled with the dust streaking the skin. Tears pricked Velma's eyes. One of the ladies placed a hand on her shoulder.

"I'm sorry my love, she's gone. Is there anyone we can get hold of for you?"

"Sam. Oh my god. Sam. He'll be waiting for us." Her hand flew to her mouth. How could she tell the boy his mother had died?

"Is that her husband?"

"No, her son. He's only nine years old. What am I going to tell him?"

A policeman appeared by her side and helped her to her feet.

"What's her name, my dear?"

"Florence. Florence Stanley. She's my sister."

"Where will you be? Is there a husband we need to contact?"

"Yes. I must go and get Sam. He'll wonder where we are. What am I going to tell him?"

"I would suggest you don't tell him anything until you're with some other member of your family. Just tell me the address of where you'll be and we'll come round to see you later."

Velma almost gave him Florence's address, but stopped. She and Sam couldn't possibly spend the night on their own. She gave the policeman Josie's address and told him they'd be spending the night there. Before she left she asked where they would take Florence's body.

"My brother-in-law will probably come and sort out the arrangements for..."

The policeman patted her shoulder to show he understood what she couldn't say. He scribbled an address on a page of his notebook, then tore it out and gave it to her.

"This is where she'll be. Give this to your brother-in-law."

She took the paper and scrunched it in her hand. With one last look at her sister's body Velma walked quickly away. She wiped her face with her handkerchief and tried to repair the ravages of her tears. She needed to get Sam to Josie to tell her older sister what had happened before they told Sam anything.

"Hello Aunty Vee, where's Mum?" Sam greeted her.

"She's still at work." Velma hated lying to him. She couldn't face telling him the truth here in the middle of the street. "We'll go on to Aunty Josie's and have tea."

Sam, content with her explanation, skipped ahead of her as they made their way to Josie's. Velma heard Josie talking cheerfully to the boy as she made her way towards the kitchen. She would have to get her sister on her own. Josie would probably scream or faint when she heard the awful news. Tom's deep voice joined in and Velma sighed with relief.

"Hello, everyone." She knew her smile must look feeble and she tried to make it seem nothing had gone wrong.

"Where's Florence?" Josie placed a weak cup of tea in front of her nephew,

"She's at work," Sam spoke through a mouthful of bread. "She won't be long, will she Aunty Vee?"

Velma shook her head, unable to speak. She had to get Tom alone without alerting Josie to her distress.

"I'll make the tea." Josie bustled out into the kitchen.

"Tom. Do you think I could have a word?" Velma flicked her gaze towards Sam.

"Of course you can, love. I'm going to have a look at my veggies. Why don't you come, too?"

Standing by the vegetable garden Velma tried several times to speak. Her voice failed her.

"Velma, is it Jack? Has something happened to Jack?" Tom placed his arm around her shoulders.

"Not Jack. It's Florence." Velma managed to gasp. "Accident. She's dead, Tom. How can I tell Sam his mother's dead?"

With low, gentle questions, Tom drew the details from her. She mentioned the policeman would be calling round later and she'd said he, Tom, would go to make the necessary arrangements. He nodded. She handed him the screwed up piece of paper in her hand.

"They said this is where she'll be."

"Leave it with me. Ask Josie if she'll come out and show me the marrow she wants me to cut. I'll tell her. I think we should talk to George before we speak to Sam. He might want to tell the boy himself."

Operating in a haze Velma did as he asked and Josie marched outside, muttering about men not being able to tie their shoelaces without help.

"What does Aunty Josie mean?" Sam wanted to know. "Can't Uncle Tom tie his shoelaces? I can do mine."

"She's just muttering, Sam. Would you like a cup of cocoa?" Velma would do anything to get out of the room.

Through the kitchen window she could see Josie being held by Tom. Her sister cried on her husband's shoulder and Velma longed for Jack to be here. He would make everything better. How silly that sounded. Nobody could make this horrible situation better. Florence had died and they had to tell George and Sam.

Tom went off to talk to the police and to arrange for the body to be brought to George and Florence's house the following day. He promised to go to Enid's to let her know what had happened. Presumably Enid would let the rest of the family know and the sisters would gather to prepare the body for burial.

Velma sent Sam to the parlour to do his homework.

"You don't want to have to do it while your Dad's home."

Josie busied herself in the kitchen so Sam couldn't see her unhappiness. Velma knew she must keep her feelings hidden for the boy's sake. Tom returned in time for the meal and they sat around the table.

"Aren't we going to wait for mum?" Sam wanted to know.

"I forgot to tell you, I spoke to her earlier. She said to tell you she's got to work really late." Velma quietly sighed with relief when Tom spoke before the women could react. "I said Sam and Velma could stay here tonight as she didn't know what time she'd be finished."

"We'll put something by for her," Velma's words successfully covered the sob Josie tried to hide.

"Can I listen to the wireless before I go to bed?"

"Have you finished your homework?" Sam nodded and Velma smiled. "Just for a little while then."

Sam huddled beside the wireless in the parlour and the adults shared a rare pot of tea around the kitchen table.

"They couldn't get hold of George. He'd already left to come home," Tom told them. "I'll meet him off the train and tell him. Enid sent her girls round to the other sisters to let them know. I think we should let George tell

Sam."

Velma hardly slept that night. Her mind kept playing over and over the scene of the van toppling onto the women. She had no idea how George would take the news. Poor man. He expected to come home and spend a weekend with his family. Instead he'd be burying his wife.

"Oh, Jack," she sobbed into her pillow. "I need you. I need to feel your arms around me and know that you can make it all right."

She knew how silly that sounded, but Velma couldn't help herself. She'd lost her beloved sister and her husband fought the enemy on the other side of the world. Despite belonging to such a big family, she had never been so alone.

*****

The next evening Velma sat in her room at Josie's writing a letter to Jack.

*...It's so awful Jack. Poor George expected to spend a happy weekend with Florence and Sam. Instead, he had to break the news to Sam that his mother had been killed. I'm staying with Josie for a few nights to give him and Sam time on their own. Then I think Sam will come to stay with Josie when I go back off my weekend leave. Oh, Jack, I miss you so much. I wish you were here with me. This is the first death we've had in the family and I hope to God it's the last one. I think the worst thing is that it happened to Florence. She only became involved in the war to do the work of a man so he could be released for active service. Take care, my love, and write soon.*

*All my love, Velma*

She placed the letter in an envelope, addressed and sealed it then sat quietly with it in her hands. Tears dripped down her cheeks and chin until they fell to the table. Quickly she moved the letter before they could blotch the ink. Would this war ever really end? And would Jack come home unscathed or would he be wounded physically or mentally like so many returning servicemen?

# Chapter Seventeen

*October 1944*

Jack sat with Velma's letter in his hand, his mind in turmoil as he tried to absorb the news it contained. How could Florence be dead? He would have understood if it had been George or any of his other brothers. Fighting the enemy brought with it certain dangers and death always lurked, waiting for the chance to step in. But Florence. She had been such a gentle soul. Her whole world had been wrapped up in her husband and son. Why had she been taken in such a way? He glanced at the date of the letter. It had taken a long while to reach him. Florence had been dead for some months.

"Something wrong, mate?" Concern rang in Pete's voice.

"My sister-in-law's been killed." Even saying the words out loud didn't make it real. "My brother George's wife, Florence. She's also Velma's sister."

"That's tough, Jack. They say Hitler is sending over flying bombs now. Doodlebugs some people call them. Did one those get her?"

"No. A stupid accident. Some idiot going too fast in a van and didn't take the corner properly. He flipped and smashed down on a group of women. A few were hurt but he killed Florence. The only one to die apparently."

"Bet your Velma is upset, it being her sister."

"Yes, she is." Jack sighed. "God, I wish this war would finish. It's not right for families to be apart at times like these. Velma needs me and so does George, yet what am I doing? Sitting here in Burma with all the luxuries of home."

"I'd hardly call mosquitoes and malaria luxuries," Pete snorted. "But I know what you mean. We've been away for years and it's time we went home. Rumours say we're winning both here and in Europe so fingers crossed it won't be long before we're on the ship homeward bound."

Jack nodded absentmindedly, his thoughts on Velma in England. At least she hadn't had to cope alone. She had her family around her and they would all pull together to take care of Sam.

The months passed, Christmas came and went. Jack's division stayed in Burma as the Allies gradually reclaimed the country from the Japanese. He wrote to Velma as often as he could. He had no idea if his letters were reaching her as he received no replies.

Frustration with the war in the Far East sent anger churning in his stomach. Neither side made any headway, both enemy and allies fighting fiercely to retain what they held. If something didn't happen soon he'd go mad.

The winter months were hell. Rain and mud made moving difficult and Jack wondered if he'd ever be dry again. Malaria struck him down twice. He recovered but the experience left him feeling washed out and sorry for himself. If only the war would end and let him go home to Velma.

\*\*\*\*\*

*August 1945*

Rumours of some hush hush event circulated. Everyone knew something big brewed. Some wondered if it might be a new weapon, others there would be an offensive launched from China. All were guesses. The excitement mounted. Could this be the big break in the stalemate?

"Jack, did you hear?" Pete shook Jack's shoulder, waking him from a heavenly dream of holding Velma in his arms.

"What? Did you have to wake me?" Jack struggled to sit up and rubbed his eyes to rid them of the last remnants of sleep.

"They did it, Jack. Those Americans did it."

"Did what? What are you blathering about, Pete?"

"They dropped a big one on Hiroshima."

"When you say big one, what exactly do you mean?" Jack asked cautiously. "And where the heck is Hiroshima?"

"An atomic bomb, Jack. They say it blew the place to smithereens and Hiroshima is a really big place. Killed thousands in the city. The Russians have joined in the war, too. It will be over before we know it."

Although glad the fighting might soon be over, Jack couldn't help feeling sorry for the loss of life in Japan. A city would have people like his family going about their daily work. They were probably loyal to their country, not involved with the actual fighting. Ordinary people died when their leaders took them to war.

Within days Jack's company moved. The Japanese had surrendered. Jack ended up in Singapore where he and his fellow RASC friends boarded the ship to take them home. They heard Hitler had committed suicide, leaving the Germans to retreat inside their own borders and surrender to the Allies.

Delighted as they were with the European war news, the troops were mainly interested in getting home to see their loved ones. It had been a long time since they'd seen mothers, sisters, wives, children and other relatives. Now they could see the beginning of the end, had Jack hoped he and Velma could start their lives afresh in a world too frightened of the consequences to start another war.

The convoy had reached the Atlantic Ocean when Jack woke one morning, shivering. His heart sank. He recognised the malaria symptoms running through his body.

"Hey, Jack, are you feeling all right?" Pete frowned at him, a concerned expression on his face. "You look terrible mate."

"Malaria," Jack managed to croak. Fever had now joined the shivering and he could feel himself slipping away.

"Hold on, Jack, I'll get the MO."

By the time his friend returned with the Medical Officer, Jack had difficulty concentrating on his surroundings. He barely felt the prick in his arm as the fever shook him to the core and his consciousness sank into blackness. As he slipped away he heard the doctor's voice.

"He's bad. I'm not sure if he'll survive this."

*****

*September 1945*

Velma frowned with worry. She hadn't heard from Jack for some time. The Wrens had been told they would be discharged over a period of months. She hoped she would get out early as she would like to be out of the service by the time Jack returned. The lack of news worried her. She tried to tell herself the erratic post must be the cause, he'd written but the letters hadn't got through. If she'd read his hints correctly, he'd been in the Far East so it would take a while for him to get home now the war had finished.

"Wren Stanley."

"Yes ma'am." Velma straightened to attention and saluted her senior officer.

"Report to the Leading Wren immediately."

Velma gave another crisp salute before hurrying to the Leading Wren's office. Several of her friends waited outside the door. Charlotte came to stand beside her.

"Do you think we're going to be sent somewhere?" she asked in a whisper.

"I hope not. My Jack might be home any day now," Velma replied.

All the women snapped to attention when the Leading Wren opened her office door. The senior officer inspected their overall appearance and then told them to stand at ease.

"As you have no doubt heard, the war is over. This means those of you who joined to help the war effort, rather than make the navy a career, will be gradually discharged. You ladies are the first ones to be released. At the end of the week you may return to your civilian lives. I thank you all for your efforts during the last years of turmoil and wish you well in your future lives."

Warmth, happiness and excitement built up inside Velma. Her own personal war had stopped. Now she could return to her family and build a new life with Jack. Hopefully, they would be able to start a family and get a home not necessarily in that order. She could hardly wait for the week to be over.

The days flew by. Addresses were exchanged between friends. Regulation issue items were cleaned and repaired before being returned to the stores. All work had to be up to date to pass on to those who were to take over from those who were leaving.

At last the release day arrived and Velma left the base in civilian clothes. The strangeness of knowing she no longer had to obey orders made her fidget. She wondered if she could get her old job back. Then doubts set in. Where would she and Jack be living? Until he returned she would be very much in limbo. He might want to live near his family. She gave a happy grin. It would all work out. As soon as Jack came home, everything would be all right. Without him she felt like a ship adrift at sea. He was her anchor, her reason for living.

Sam had been staying with Josie and Tom once George returned to his unit. The boy had understandably been upset by the loss of his mother. Despite this he got on with life, except when his young face took on a sad and thoughtful expression.

"I'm free," Velma called laughingly as she walked into Josie's kitchen. "No longer Wren Stanley, I'm now just plain Mrs. Jack Stanley."

"Are we going to celebrate?" Sam looked up expectantly from where he sat at the kitchen table.

"What a good idea. What shall we do?"

Velma smiled at Josie as Sam thoughtfully sucked his pencil, trying to think of what would be the best way to celebrate Velma's discharge.

"Can we catch the ferry over to Torpoint and have a picnic?"

"I think we can manage that, don't you, Josie? We'll go tomorrow." Velma smiled at her sister and sighed with relief when Josie returned her smile. All the family missed Florence, but Josie took it to heart more than the others. Especially now she had sole care of Sam.

The next day they packed up as good a picnic as the rationing would allow. Sam had this week's sweet ration. Enid had given them some lemons from her garden so they were able to make a small amount of lemonade to take with them.

Despite it being Saturday, Tom had to work so only the three of them set out for the Plymouth side of the ferry terminal. Velma normally considered the ferries to be smelly and noisy. Today, with Sam's cheerful voice pointing out things to see in the water and on the shore, it didn't bother her quite so much.

They stood side-by-side watching the chains clanking and disappearing underneath as it pulled the ferry from one bank to the other. Velma and Josie followed an excited Sam as they disembarked on the Cornwall side. They had a lovely time investigating a place they were not too familiar with. Velma had been through Torpoint several times while in the Wrens, but had never had time to stop and take in the sights.

"How about here for our picnic?" Josie suggested when they came to a small park. "It's nice and quiet and Sam can kick his football around without bothering anyone."

The boy had insisted on bringing the ball with him, despite Josie telling him he'd have no one to play with. The women laid out the food on a blanket and then sat back to enjoy the warm sunshine. Velma watched Sam desultory kicking the ball around. Poor boy, she decided to do something to cheer him up.

"Come on, football star, put some effort into it." Velma stood and moved across the field. "Kick it this way."

Sam took up her challenge and for several minutes the ball passed rapidly between them.

"Let's make a goal, Aunty Vee. Then I can try and shoot past you."

Velma and Sam's sweaters became the goalposts. She stood waiting while the boy dribbled the ball towards her. From the way he kept looking at her she knew he would shoot to her right. She didn't want to spoil his fun by stopping the ball so she deliberately dived to the left. The ball shot past her.

"Goal!" Sam shouted and did a war dance of excitement.

Exhausted, Velma and Sam flopped down on the grass when Josie called to them to take time to eat.

"When are Dad and Uncle Jack coming home?" Sam took a huge bite of his sandwich. "The war is supposed to be over so shouldn't they be home?"

"Don't talk with your mouth full," Josie scolded. "It depends on when they get de-mobbed. Some services take longer than others. We'll probably hear from your Dad sometime in the next week. How about Jack, Velma?"

"I'm not sure. I expect he's on his way home from the Far East by now, unless of course there's a shortage of ships."

They finished eating and packed away the remains of the picnic. Velma held her hand out and small droplets of water hit her palm.

"I think it's starting to rain. We'd better get back to the ferry. We can shelter there."

The rain fell heavier by the time they reached the terminal. Luckily, a ferry had just arrived and they hurried on board.

"Well Sam, did you enjoy yourself?" Velma asked as they settled in their seats.

"Great. I really enjoyed playing football with you, Aunty Vee. Can we do it again when Dad and Uncle Jack are here?"

"I don't see why not."

The ferry clanked to a stop on the Plymouth side and they picked up the bags and disembarked.

"Oh no, it's still raining." Josie frowned. "We'll be soaked by the time we get home."

"Never mind, a little bit of rain never hurt anyone." Velma couldn't explain it. A sudden feeling of light heartedness made her want to skip for joy. "We can all dry off when we get home. It's not cold."

The weather eased a little while they waited for the bus. By the time they got off near the house, the rain poured down again.

They reached the end of their road and Sam ran on ahead. He stopped as a man stepped out from the shadows by their front door. Josie gasped and ran down the street in an effort to protect Sam. Velma stood frozen to the spot.

Josie spoke a few words to the man then hurried Sam inside the house.

The man turned and looked directly at Velma. At first she didn't know for sure. He'd lost so much weight and the clothes hung off him. Plus, she'd never seen him out of uniform. He smiled and her doubts disappeared. He opened his arms to her.

Slowly, her feet moved one step at a time down the street, each step faster than the previous one until she fairly flew down the road.

"Jack. Oh, Jack."

She rushed into his arms and they folded round her. Snuggling close to him she heard the beat of his heart. The familiar smell of his shaving soap tickled her nose. Her head fitted into its proper place beneath his chin. Jack's arms were home for her. She tightened her grip round his body. Gently, he placed a hand under her chin and lifted her face until she could see the smile on his lips.

"Is it really you? I'm not dreaming, am I?"

"No, Velma, you're not dreaming. I'm home at last and I'm never going to leave you again."

Velma reached up and pulled his head down to hers. Their lips met, softly at first, then more passionately as they made up for their years apart. The kiss lasted for several minutes, and when they eventually stopped, Jack took her hand and together they walked into the house, ready to start their future together.

*The End*

## About Sue Perkins

Sue Perkins was born in England, and her husband's job enabled them to travel around the world. After the children were born the family moved to Kuwait and then on to New Zealand while the children were still young.

Over twenty years later Sue and her husband still live in the South Island of New Zealand. Sue's first novel was published in 1997, followed by several more fantasy and romance books over the ensuing years. Many more stories are clamoring to be written, so look out for Sue Perkins books and enjoy.

Read more about Sue at http://www.SuePerkinsAuthor.com

Printed in Great Britain
by Amazon